"You _____ *?* asked with a sexy chuckle.*

"Of you? I most certainly am not!"

"Maybe you're afraid of the way I make you feel." She heard him laugh again, that low laugh that made her tingle with a primitive sexual excitement. "It's quite normal, you know. Women are often afraid of the men they're powerfully attracted to."

"And from where do you draw your facts?" she demanded hotly. Her whole body was one heated blush. She refused to admit it, but his suggestive supposition actually made sense to her in an odd sort of way.

"I made them up," he replied cheerfully.

"Oh! You!" Juliet glared at Caine with all the wrath she could muster. "You're—you're—" Why did she have to become incoherent at a time like this? No doubt the cleverly scathing retort she longed to throw at him would occur to her tomorrow.

"I'm going to pick you up at seven-fifteen," Caine said casually, then paused to fix his deep amber eyes on her blue ones. "I could make your head spin in bed, Juliet," he drawled softly. "Are you going to let me?"

WHAT ARE *LOVESWEPT* ROMANCES?

They are stories of true romance and touching emotion. We believe those two very important ingredients are constants in our highly sensual and very believable stories in the *LOVESWEPT* line. Our goal is to give you, the reader, stories of consistently high quality that may sometimes make you laugh, sometimes make you cry, but are always fresh and creative and contain many delightful surprises within their pages.

Most romance fans read an enormous number of books. Those they truly love, they keep. Others may be traded with friends and soon forgotten. We hope that each *LOVESWEPT* romance will be a treasure—a "keeper." We will always try to publish

LOVE STORIES YOU'LL NEVER FORGET
BY AUTHORS YOU'LL ALWAYS REMEMBER

The Editors

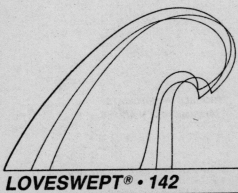

LOVESWEPT® • 142

Barbara Boswell
Trouble in Triplicate

 BANTAM BOOKS
TORONTO • NEW YORK • LONDON • SYDNEY • AUCKLAND

TROUBLE IN TRIPLICATE
A Bantam Book / May 1986

ISBN 0-553-21754-2

Published simultaneously in the United States and Canada

Bantam Books are published by Bantam Books, Inc. Its
trademark, consisting of the words "Bantam Books" and
the portrayal of a rooster, is Registered in U.S. Patent and
Trademark Office and in other countries. Marca Registrada.
Bantam Books, Inc., 666 Fifth Avenue, New York, New
York 10103.

PRINTED IN THE UNITED STATES OF AMERICA

O   0 9 8 7 6 5 4 3 2 1

One

"You did that deliberately, didn't you?" The deep, masculine voice sounded in Juliet Post's ear, and she whirled around to find herself facing Caine Saxon, the brother of the one true enemy she possessed in this world. She decided that made him an enemy-by-association.

"You!" Juliet glowered at him. "What are *you* doing here?" Fate had never been unkind enough to throw them together socially . . . until now, it seemed. Here they were at the Wilmonts' party, just a few inches apart in the noisy, crowded living room. And then another, more troubling thought struck. "Is your brother here too?"

Juliet cast an anxious glance toward the kitchen, where her sisters were preparing trays of hot hors d'oeuvres to be served to the party guests. John and Laura Wilmont had hired the Post Sisters' Catering Service for the evening. What if Grant Saxon *were* here? With another woman? How would Randi react to that? Not well, Juliet feared. Her sister was having a rough time getting over that lying, cheating, bestial Grant Saxon. And here *she* was, face to face with his odious brother.

Caine didn't look particularly thrilled to see her, either. "No, Grant isn't here." He scowled at her. "Well, which one are you? Juliet, Miranda, or Olivia?"

Juliet scowled back at him. Life as an identical triplet had taught her to be tolerant of those who couldn't tell her apart from her two sisters, but she was unable to indulge Caine Saxon with her usual patience in the matter. "It's none of your business who I am!" she snapped.

"Juliet, Miranda, and Olivia." Caine shook his head as he repeated the names. "Right out of Shakespeare, huh?"

"Our parents were English professors here at U. Va." She'd told the story of their names so many times, it was natural to lapse into it. And then she remembered that she was talking to the enemy, and she frowned. "I'm amazed that you've even heard of Shakespeare. After all, he had nothing to do with football."

Caine grinned in spite of himself. "Yeah, if *I* had triplets, I'd name them O. J., Bradshaw, and Bart Starr." And then he remembered that he was talking to the enemy and his expression hardened. "So are you going to tell me which one you are?"

"No," Juliet replied succinctly.

"Then I'll just have to figure it out for myself, won't I?" Caine's gaze swept over her, taking in her slender five-foot-four height; her short dark hair, which framed her small face like a sleek, smooth cap; her big, wide-set eyes, which were a deep periwinkle blue in color. Her small, straight nose with its slight smattering of freckles gave her a wholesome girl-next-door look, and she had a firm little chin and a sweetly generous mouth.

She was slim and small-boned and lovely—and she had two sisters who looked exactly like her.

Confusion flickered across Caine's face. He couldn't tell one sister from the other. He'd never been able to.

"Doesn't it spook you?" he'd once asked his brother Grant during Grant's whirlwind courtship of Miranda Post. "The Post triplets are clones of each other. Isn't it weird to be with a woman who's interchangeable with two others?" Caine couldn't fathom it. He knew he'd always wonder which was the original. And suppose they tricked you with a substitute?

Grant had merely laughed. "There are ways of telling the triplets apart," he'd said, amused. "Their personalities are totally different. I guess that's the most reliable way of knowing who is who."

Caine decided to use that clue to learn this particular Post's identity now. "If you won't tell me who you are, I'll find out by process of elimination." His brows narrowed in concentration. "Olivia is never without her trusty sidekick, Bobby Lee Taggert. There is no Bobby Lee by your side, so you can't be Olivia. Miranda is so quiet that she doesn't speak until she's spoken to. You certainly haven't been quiet and shy, so unless Miranda has undergone a radical personality change since she broke up with my brother, you can't be her. That leaves me with Juliet, the acknowledged leader of the pack. You're Juliet, aren't you?"

"You're a regular sleuth, Sherlock."

"I like to know the identity of the person I'm speaking to." Caine's momentary smile of triumph faded, to be replaced by a frown. "You did it deliberately, didn't you, Juliet?"

"What are you talking about?" she asked with unconcealed irritation.

"I saw you introduce that scholarly looking guy to my date!"

Juliet followed his gaze to a corner of the room

where her friend and neighbor, Mark Walsh—who wore wire-rimmed glasses, was a math professor at the university, and was both scholarly looking and brilliant—was talking to a lovely blonde. Juliet had introduced him to her ten minutes before.

"That's Sherry Carson, the weather girl on Channel 42," Juliet said aloud. Sherry Carson was Mark's dream girl, and he'd nearly swooned when he'd seen her here at the party. He was too shy and nervous to introduce himself to the star of his fantasies, so Juliet had introduced herself to Sherry, and then introduced Sherry to Mark.

"I know it's Sherry Carson," Caine said impatiently. "I was the one who brought her to this party."

"She was standing alone when I introduced myself to her. And she seemed happy to have some company," Juliet retorted. "She said that she didn't know anyone here and she appeared to be very pleased to meet Mark."

"She was angry with me because I'd left her alone too long to talk football with some of the guys."

They watched Sherry Carson talking animatedly to Mark Walsh, who appeared to be listening raptly. "They seem to be getting along very well," Juliet said. "Too bad, Mr. Saxon. Looks like you've lost your date."

Juliet was delighted at the turn of events. She was pleased that Mark seemed to be making headway with the girl of his dreams, and she relished the fact that Caine Saxon's date had defected—thanks to the matchmaking efforts of Juliet Post.

"You're feeling quite pleased with yourself, aren't you?" Caine said. "The expression on your face is a dead giveaway. You look like Sylvester the Cat grinning at Tweety Bird as Grandma departs for the day."

"I can't take full credit." Juliet shrugged. "Mark Walsh is as sweet and sincere as you Saxons are cold and shallow and deceitful. It shouldn't take Sherry Carson long to realize that."

"Sherry isn't the sweet and sincere type. And I resent your slur on the collective Saxon character, lady."

"It's not a slur, it's a statement of fact!"

Caine's eyes glittered. "You're lucky you're a woman, Ms. Post. Because if you were a man, I'd—"

"You'd what? Meet me outside and take me apart limb by limb?" Juliet asked mockingly. "Your stupid machismo is out of date, Saxon. A real man doesn't have to fight to prove his manhood these days. Or womanize, either. Of course, I wouldn't expect you or your conniving brother to know anything about men with values and morals. That's alien territory for you, isn't it?"

Caine was clearly angry. His body was taut and his eyes flashed fire. Obviously, she'd struck a nerve. Juliet congratulated herself.

"Grant told me how impossible you three clones have been! He said there's no reasoning with any of you, and I can see he's right." Caine's voice was low and husky with intensity. "Well, you've got one helluva nerve, lady! Especially since it was your sister who jilted my brother!"

"*After* she found out he was cheating on her! I'd say she was quite justified in breaking their engagement."

Caine was briefly taken aback. "Cheated on her? Is that why she ended the engagement?"

"I know it must come as a great surprise to a couple of swinging playboys like you and your brother, but most women believe that when a man proposes marriage—and goes so far as to buy an engagement ring—he is ready and willing to give up other women. But not Grant Saxon!" Juliet clenched her fists. "Two weeks before his wedding *he* goes to Richmond and spends the weekend with another woman! Can you blame Randi for calling off the wedding? What kind of a husband would your brother make if he—"

"Julie, we need some help with the lamb in the kitchen." The young woman who joined them at that moment was Juliet's duplicate, from the gold hoop earrings affixed to her small earlobes to the white over-sized shirt belted at the waist with a wide bright blue belt to the white cropped slacks, bright blue shoes, and gold ankle bracelet.

"I'm coming, Livvy," Juliet said tightly, scarcely glancing at her sister.

For a dazed moment Caine wondered how she knew which sister it was. He blinked, and the two sisters turned and started toward the kitchen. He stared after them and wondered which was the one he'd been talking to. Quarreling with, he silently amended. And there were *three* of them!

He gave his head a slight shake, as if to clear it. They spooked him, all right. Poor Grant might not realize it now, but he'd had a lucky escape from that crew! In addition to being unnervingly identical, they were vengeful and vindictive.

For one solid month Grant had suffered through having the phone slammed down in his ear, having his letters returned unopened, and his flowers returned with the cards torn into pieces. All this from the woman who had jilted *him!* And now it appeared that the triple threat had declared war on all Saxons. Juliet had undoubtedly seen him come into the Wilmonts' house with Sherry Carson and set out to sabotage his date by introducing her to another man.

Caine glanced across the room to where Mark Walsh was gazing at Sherry Carson with unadulterated adoration. The way that Grant used to gaze at Miranda Post, Caine thought grimly. Well, it appeared he'd lost Sherry to the young scholar in the wire-rimmed glasses. It bothered him a little that he didn't care at all, but he didn't. There had already been quite a few Sherry Carson types in his life, brief flings who accepted and promised nothing but a good time and no strings attached.

Perhaps Sherry had decided that Mark Walsh's undisguised admiration was a better deal than Caine Saxon's undisguised indifference. Chalk one up for Juliet Post for providing the means for her defection.

Saxon—zero, Post—one, he mentally scored. Or was it Post—two? Miranda's outright, abject rejection of Grant certainly counted for something. Poor Grant. Caine grimaced as he visualized the dejected countenance his brother wore these days. The Saxon brothers weren't accustomed to outright, abject rejection by anyone, let alone by a woman! Since their grade-school days, when they'd played midget football, they'd been popular with the girls.

Playboys, Juliet Post had scathingly called them. Caine didn't care for the term. To him, it conjured up an image of a smarmy Latin lover in a velvet smoking jacket with rings on his fingers. He and Grant had dated a lot of women between them, but they'd never resorted to velvet smoking jackets, jewels, and smarminess.

The Post triplets were small-town girls, he reminded himself. They'd been born and raised here in Charlottesville, Virginia, and were still here at the age of twenty-six. The fact that he and Grant had been nationally known pro football players and lived in big cities—himself in Pittsburgh and Grant in Atlanta—undoubtedly made them seem cosmopolitan and sophisticated to a provincial trio like the Post sisters.

"Randi, I don't want to upset you," Juliet said. In the spacious Wilmont kitchen she was helping her sisters transfer the side of roast lamb from the roaster to the serving board. "But that jerk Caine Saxon is here tonight."

Miranda paled slightly. "Is—Is *he* here too?"

"Grant? No, at least we've been spared that misery." Juliet watched her sister with concern. Poor Randi! she thought. She hadn't been eating or sleeping well since her breakup with Grant Saxon, and she always seemed on the verge of tears.

A wave of pure rage surged through Juliet. A month ago Randi had been happily anticipating her wedding, wildly and crazily in love with Charlottesville's own hometown football hero, Grant Saxon. And for the first time in her life, Randi—"the shy one, the quiet one," as people insisted upon labeling her—had been confident and vibrant, sure of her worth as an individual rather than as part of a matched set of three. And then Grant Saxon had taken it all away from her, had smashed her dreams and self-confidence to smithereens.

"Hey, Julie, watch it, girl!" Bobby Lee Taggert, Olivia's boyfriend—sidekick, Caine Saxon had called him—grinned at her. "You're making me nervous, waving that carvin' knife like a pirate about to slash someone's throat."

Juliet couldn't help but grin back. Bobby Lee was always even-tempered, good-humored, and marvelously uncomplicated. Probably from growing up in the middle of a farm family of nine children, the sisters had decided. He was the manager of the Charlottesville Safeway, the local branch of the national supermarket chain. He cheerfully tagged along with Olivia and was so comfortable with the triplets that they sometimes joked that he'd been quadruplets with them in some past lifetime. He and Olivia were saving for the down payment on a house before they married. Olivia's idea, which Bobby Lee accepted with his usual good cheer.

"What did you say to Caine Saxon, Julie?" Olivia asked. "Both of you were glaring at each other like—like—"

"Two hound dogs squaring off to fight?" Bobby Lee supplied helpfully.

Olivia smiled at him. "Exactly."

"I was just pointing out a few home truths to Snake Saxon," Juliet said as she scooped mint jelly into a china bowl. "What a fitting nickname! When the press started calling him 'Snake' because he was such a hotshot wide receiver in the pros, I wonder if they realized what an apt name they'd chosen?"

"They should've called Grant 'Rat,'" Olivia added loyally.

"Julie, did he . . . did Caine . . . mention"— Miranda swallowed hard and her voice lowered— "anything about Grant?"

Juliet scowled. "He expressed surprise that you'd broken your engagement simply because Grant had spent the weekend in Richmond with that woman. I guess the Saxon brothers feel they're such great prizes that a woman would put up with anything just for the privilege of marrying one of them."

"Not me," Miranda whispered. "Oh, Julie, oh, Livvy, what a fool I was to get involved with Grant in the first place! I knew all about his reputation the first time I went out with him. He was a pro football player, and women had been throwing themselves at him for years. But he said he'd changed. He said that since he'd retired from the NFL and come home to Charlottesville, he'd wanted to settle down and start a family. . . ." Tears darkened her deep blue eyes to a violet shade and her voice trailed off.

"Isn't there some down-home metaphor about rodents and reptiles never changing their spots?" Juliet asked Bobby Lee.

"I think it's leopards," Bobby Lee said. "And we don't have them down on the farm."

"Why did Grant and Caine Saxon have to come back to Charlottesville, anyway?" Olivia lamented. "Why couldn't they have opened their stupid restaurant in some other town?"

"Because washed-up pro football players are a dime a dozen, Livvy," Juliet said. "Where else would they be the celebrities they are here in Charlottesville?" She tossed the spinach salad with unaccustomed force. "Their restaurant would never have been the smash success it's been in any place *but* their old hometown!"

"I don't know about that, Julie." Bobby Lee looked thoughtful. "I mean, the restaurant is a huge hit with the university crowd and they have no hometown sentiment for the Saxon brothers. The food at The Knight Out is good and cheap, and that Middle-Ages decor of theirs is real original, and—"

"*The Knight Out!*" Juliet grinned in spite of herself. "Doesn't the name fracture you? The typical choice of two moronic ex-jocks."

"Let's not talk about them anymore," Miranda murmured in a strangled voice. She was obviously fighting back tears, and Juliet felt a sharp pain of her own at the sight of her sister's misery. It had always been so, from the time the triplets were toddlers. If one of them was hurt, the other two cried too.

Bobby Lee was fully aware of it. "Come on, let's get this lamb out to the hungry masses." He lifted the large serving board. "Livvy, get the door for me, darlin'."

Olivia preceded Bobby Lee out of the kitchen. Juliet turned to Miranda and laid a sisterly arm around her shoulders. "I wish I could help, Randi," she whispered fervently. "I wish I could make everything all right for you again."

Miranda managed a watery smile. "I know, Julie." She gave Juliet a quick, hard hug. "I know."

When the phone rang at eleven o'clock the next morning Juliet was the only one at home to answer it. Bobby Lee had come by an hour earlier to take Olivia shopping, and they'd coaxed Miranda into going along. Juliet had stayed behind to bake a triple fudge cake that a customer had ordered for a birthday party that night.

She had just placed the three layers on separate cooling racks when the phone began to ring. "Post Sisters' Catering Service," she said briskly into the phone.

"I'd like to speak to Miranda, please."

Juliet's heart somersaulted in her chest. She recognized the voice at once. It was Caine Saxon. After a momentary pause she replied, "This is Miranda Post speaking."

She was acting in Randi's best interests, she assured herself. She was sparing her sister the emotional pain of dealing with yet another Saxon. The fact that she was shamefully curious as to why Caine was calling Randi might also be involved in her deception, she acknowledged dryly.

Caine paused a moment too. Then he said, "Miranda, this is Caine Saxon. I'd like to talk to you."

"I'm listening," Juliet said coolly.

"Not over the phone. In person. May I come over?"

"I really don't think that's a good idea, Mr. Saxon."

"You used to call me Caine." His voice was soft, and then suddenly suspicious. "Is this really Miranda? Or one of the others impersonating her?"

Juliet didn't care for his phrasing. "One of the

others," he'd said, and rather scornfully too! As if she were part of a litter or something! "If you want to see me, I'm free now," she said coldly.

There was a long pause on Caine's end of the line. "All right . . . Miranda. It's quite important that I speak with you. I'll be right over."

She was nervous, Juliet conceded as she glanced into the bathroom mirror a few minutes later. She picked up a comb and ran it through her hair. Even as she was applying her makeup she was admonishing herself for doing it. Why should she care what she looked like for this meeting with Caine Saxon? She resolutely refused to answer that silent question.

She was wearing a pair of tight, faded jeans and a navy University of Virginia sweat shirt with the sleeves cut off to the elbow, and she wondered if she should change clothes. And immediately decided against it. She had to draw the line somewhere! She would *not* get dressed up for a Saxon!

Fifteen minutes later she peered out the window to see a canary yellow Ferrari pull up in front of the Posts' small frame house. Caine Saxon climbed out, moving with the lithe grace of a natural athlete. Juliet watched him as he strode purposefully up the front walk. He was wearing jeans, too, and a white polo shirt bearing the Pittsburgh Steelers logo. Shades of past glory, Juliet thought with a sniff. But she couldn't seem to take her eyes from him as he walked to her door.

He was so big, at least six-foot-four, and his body was powerfully built, all hard muscled strength without an ounce of excess weight. The body of a professional athlete still, although he'd retired from his position as wide receiver for the Pittsburgh Steelers at the end of last season. This was his first fall as a Charlottesville restaurateur, and she wondered briefly how he was adjusting to the change in life-style. Miserably, she hoped with a flash of venom. She hoped that his perfidious brother Grant was miserable too!

She opened the front door just as he was about to knock, and they stared at each other in silence for a long moment. Caine Saxon *was* handsome, Juliet admitted grudgingly. In addition to that tall, masculine frame, nature had blessed him with thick dark hair the color of burnished chestnut, and the most unusually colored eyes that she had ever seen. They were a dark yellow-brown, an intriguing amber color that reminded her of a cat's eyes. He had a strong, square jaw and a well-shaped mouth. Bobby Lee had once remarked that Caine Saxon looked like the cowboy hero in one of those old Western movies.

But he was no hero, Juliet reminded herself sternly. He was a rat by association with his brother.

"Miranda?" Caine asked uncertainly.

"Or one of the others impersonating her?" she said waspishly.

"I'm sorry about that." He looked a bit sheepish. "But I had to know if I really was talking to Miranda. You see, I'm very worried about my brother."

Juliet froze. "Has—has something happened to Grant?" As much as she loathed the man for what he'd done to her sister, she didn't really wish him physical harm, Juliet realized with some surprise.

"May I come in? I don't care to discuss it on the front porch."

Juliet led him into the small living room and sat down on the blue-and-yellow-striped couch. When Caine sat down beside her she resisted the urge to move to another chair across the room. It was because he was so big and she was so hostile to him that she was so disconcertingly aware of him sitting beside her, she told herself. He seemed to dwarf the couch, the entire room, by his presence.

"What happened to Grant?" she asked, her voice suddenly breathless.

"You happened to Grant, Miranda. He fell in love with you and planned to spend the rest of his life with you. And then, without rhyme or reason, you called off the wedding."

"Without rhyme or reason? The fact that he spent a weekend in Richmond with another woman two weeks before the wedding isn't rhyme or reason enough?"

"Miranda, do you know that until last night Grant didn't know why you'd broken your engagement? You refused to speak to him—you returned his ring by mail and left a message on his answering machine that you never wanted to see him again. He's tried and tried to see you, to talk to you, but you and your sisters haven't let him near you."

"There was nothing he could say that—"

"Do you realize that if I hadn't talked to that spit-fire sister of yours, he still wouldn't know why you'd called off the wedding? I told him last night that the reason you broke up with him was because he had allegedly spent an illicit weekend in Richmond with another woman."

" 'Allegedly'?" Juliet echoed crossly. "There was nothing alleged about it, mister!"

"How do you know, Miranda? You never gave the man a chance to explain. You tried, convicted, and sentenced him without ever hearing him out."

Juliet thought about that. She'd urged Randi to confront Grant, but her sister couldn't bear the thought of seeing him, of hearing his lies. Randi had never been one to quarrel. Arguing and tension and raised voices could literally make her sick. She'd avoided confrontations all her life, and neither Juliet nor Olivia had had the heart to force one upon her at this most stressful time in her life.

"Miranda, Grant was devastated by this

breakup. I've never seen him like this. For the past month he hasn't been sleeping well or eating well, and—"

"Well, neither has—" Uh-oh, she'd almost said Randi. And she was supposed to *be* Randi! "—uh, have I," Juliet quickly corrected herself.

Caine held her captive with his piercing amber gaze. She shifted uncomfortably, excruciatingly aware of the hard virility emanating from him. "Let me ask you just one more question, Miranda."

He leaned forward slightly, and Juliet inhaled the fresh scent of him, a heady mixture of soap and after-shave and pure male. She swallowed and forced herself to refrain from skittering away from him. Randi wouldn't skitter. Randi would be utterly immune to the potent sensual effect generated by Grant's brother. It worried Juliet that she herself was not.

"What's the question?" she asked, and her voice quavered, much to her annoyance.

"How did you learn that Grant went to Richmond that weekend with another woman? You never confronted him with it. You simply mailed him your engagement ring and left that message on his machine."

Juliet was on firm ground with this one. She knew the full story of Grant Saxon's treachery by heart. "We were catering a card party that Friday afternoon, and when we got home there was a message on *our* answering machine from your mother telling . . . me to call Grant. When I did I got *his* answering machine with the usual standard message. You know, Grant saying, 'I'm not here, please leave your name and number.' "

Juliet paused for a breath. "So I called your mother's house and your sister Sophia answered. She was very evasive when I asked about Grant. She said he wasn't there, that she thought she'd heard him say that he was going away for the weekend, but that she wasn't sure."

Juliet's eyes burned with a blue flame of anger. "Grant hadn't mentioned going away for the weekend. We—we had a date for that night! I thought maybe Sophia had gotten her facts mixed up, that maybe *you* were the one going away for the weekend, so we—the three of us—went down to your restaurant." Juliet paused, remembering the debacle that had followed. "Your mother was there. She was rather vague, but she did say that Grant had left that morning for Richmond."

"And from *that* you deduced he'd gone with another woman?" Caine asked incredulously.

"No, of course not! We assumed there must be some logical explanation—until Karen Wilbur called the next morning to say she'd seen Grant in the lobby of the Richmond Hilton the night before with a woman who wasn't Miranda!"

Caine frowned. "Karen Wilbur, that gossipy little prune! I never understood how Sophia could stand her."

"They've been best friends since junior high school," Juliet said. She didn't bother to add that she knew neither Sophia Saxon nor Karen Wilbur liked any of the Post triplets. They'd gone all through elementary school and junior and senior high schools together and had never been friends.

"So, you ended your engagement over a piece of spiteful gossip?"

"No!" Juliet glared at him. "But I was upset"—A mild understatement. Randi had been nearly catatonic with worry.—"and so Bobby Lee called your mother's house and asked to speak to Grant. Sophia answered. She assumed that Bobby was a friend of Grant's, I suppose, and she told him that he'd taken someone named Darla Ditmayer to Richmond and wouldn't be back till Sunday."

"Darla Ditmayer?"

"Grant called a few hours later. *He* said that he'd driven to Petersburg to pick up some fresh produce for the restaurant and the truck had broken down. He said it was in a Petersburg garage and he wouldn't be able to make it back until Sunday."

"Oh, boy!" Caine shook his head. "It sounds incriminating, all right. Poor Grant."

"Poor Grant? That lowlife sneaked off for a weekend with that—that Darla Ditmayer person and then lied about it!"

"Last night Grant told me that he'd never been unfaithful to you, Miranda."

"And you believed him?"

"Hell, why would he lie to me?"

"Maybe he's a compulsive liar, I don't know. We do know he lied to Randi about the weekend."

Caine tensed. "Wait a minute! *You're* supposed to be Randi!"

"Well, I'm not!" Juliet folded her arms across her chest and glared at him. "I'm her spitfire sister."

Two

"Juliet?" Caine stared at her.

"That's right."

"Damn, I should have known!" He sprang to his feet. "You tricked me! How does a person deal with someone who comes in triplicate? How does anyone ever know who is who is who?" He began to pace the floor, talking more to himself than to Juliet.

"It's downright eerie for three people to look like one! And it's unfair to everybody else! How can I be certain you're really Juliet? You could be Olivia for all I know. Or Miranda, pretending to be Juliet pretending to be Miranda!" He looked confused and flustered and utterly incensed.

Juliet tried and failed to suppress a laugh. His indignation struck her as hilarious. "You would've had a real problem with the Dionne quintuplets," she said dryly. "There were *five* of them!"

He gave her a ferocious scowl. "I like to keep the players straight on my game card."

"Is that a football metaphor?" she teased.

Caine's scowl grew even more fierce. He stopped pacing and turned to study her with accusing amber eyes. "Are you the same one I talked to on the phone earlier?"

Juliet nodded blithely.

"Why did you say you were Miranda? Or do the three of you make a practice of impersonating one another?"

"Of course not!" She paused. "Not unless it's absolutely necessary," she added defensively, avoiding his piercing eyes.

"I'd like to know what you deem a necessity. A dinner party? Why were the three of you dressed alike last night if not for the express purpose of confusing everyone?" he asked challengingly.

"Last night we were working. Those are the only times we dress alike. It's a gimmick we use. People seem intrigued by having identical triplets as their caterers, so our dressing alike is part of the service. It serves as a conversation piece and it boosts our business. At least it did when we first started four years ago. Our reputation has grown and we've enough steady customers now that I think maybe we could dispense with it, but—"

"You have too much fun driving people insane by playing guess who," he finished caustically. "Which doesn't explain why you masqueraded as your sister Miranda today."

Juliet met his gaze. "I wanted to find out what you were up to and I wanted to spare Randi the ordeal of talking to you."

"Talking to me is an ordeal?"

"For Randi it would be. She doesn't need to listen to you plead your brother's case. I want to spare her any more hurt by any more Saxons."

"Your sister hurt my brother, too, Juliet. I've never seen Grant so strung out over anyone or anything."

Juliet sniffed. "If Grant loved Randi so much,

then why would he go to Richmond with another woman two weeks before his wedding?"

"He wouldn't." Caine sat back down, frowning. "I know my brother. Grant has never been a deceitful, manipulative womanizer. Neither have I," he added with a sharp glance at Juliet.

"And I suppose all those photos of you and Grant with beauty contestants and Hollywood starlets and professional cheerleaders—the ones you have framed and hanging on the walls of your restaurant—I suppose those are all composite pictures? Because you and Grant have never—"

"I didn't say we haven't . . . uh, dated women. Of course we have. Hell, I'm thirty-four years old and Grant is thirty-three. We'd be pretty strange guys if we'd reached these ages without some . . . er, experience with the opposite sex. But we've never lied or cheated or hurt a woman. We've always been honest in our relationships. We never made promises or commitments. We always made it plain we wanted good times without serious involvement."

"Maybe you're both incapable of making a serious commitment. Grant certainly blew all the promises he made to Randi. Good-time Charlies like you and Grant should stick to the Good-Time Shirleys of the world!"

Caine heaved an exasperated sigh. "The point I'm trying to make—and the point you keep missing—is that Grant *didn't* break faith with Miranda. I know the facts seem incriminating, but . . ." His voice trailed off and he stared into space. "Something just doesn't ring true, Juliet. I sense a setup."

She rolled her eyes heavenward. "I think you've been watching too many nighttime soap operas on TV. We're not the Ewings and the Carringtons, Saxon. Who would want to cause trouble between Grant and Randi?"

Caine looked thoughtful. "The common thread

running through the entire story seems to be"—he drew in his breath sharply—"my sister Sophia."

"Sophia?" Juliet stared at him, thoroughly taken aback. Had he made some wild accusation involving herself or Olivia, she would've laughed it off—or told him off! But for him to mention his own sister . . .

"Darla Ditmayer is the daughter of a friend of my mother's—and a friend of Sophia's as well. And Karen Wilbur, who called Miranda to report having seen Grant and Darla in Richmond, is Sophia's closest friend. It was Sophia herself who acted evasive over the telephone. And it was Sophia who told Bobby Lee Taggert that Grant was in Richmond with Darla."

"It's probably just a string of coincidences. Why would Sophia want to wreck her brother's engagement?" Juliet couldn't fathom such a thing. It was difficult enough to believe that Caine was making this accusation against his own sister!

"Maybe she didn't intend to wreck his engagement. Maybe she simply intended to cause a little misery for one of the Post triplets."

"But—but why?"

"My sister has a long list of grievances against you three dating back to your grade-school days. Being eight years older than Sophia, I was never much involved with her as a child, but I do recall her lamenting over how unfair it was that you Posts had been born a trio. You triplets always had a starring number in every dancing-school recital, you were always invited to every birthday party, you took up three places on the cheerleading squad, you took up three places at Mary Washington College, thus always eliminating Sophia . . . or so she claimed."

Juliet stared at him, momentarily bereft of speech. She and her sisters had never given

Sophia Saxon a thought, and Sophia had held a grudge against them for being born triplets all these years? "It's too bizarre!" she managed to say at last. "It's easier to believe that Grant went to Richmond for a fling with Darla Ditmayer."

"Not if you knew my brother as well as I know him." Caine frowned. "As well as your sister *should* have known him. She's displayed an appalling lack of trust in Grant. I don't know if she deserves another chance with him."

"She doesn't *want* another chance with him, Saxon."

Caine ignored her. "I'm going to have a little talk with my sister this afternoon. If she confirms my suspicions, I'll be in touch with you later, Juliet. I'm afraid it will be our job to get this engagement back on the track again."

"Our job? Why on earth would I want to help your lying, cheating brother get reengaged to my sister?"

"Because he isn't a liar and a cheat. I neglected to mention one small fact to you, Juliet. On the weekend two weeks before his wedding, Grant did go to Petersburg to buy produce, and our truck did break down, forcing him to spend the weekend there. We have dated sales receipts to prove it."

Juliet's eyes widened. "But—but even your mother said he was in Richmond."

"Probably because that's what Sophia told her. And you can bet Sophia didn't mention the Darla Ditmayer part to Mom. There would've been too many questions asked."

"Does your mother hate us too?" Juliet asked quietly.

Caine shook his head. "No. She was quite pleased when Grant and Miranda got engaged. Another thorn in Sophia's side, I guess."

Juliet sank down onto the sofa. "I can't believe Sophia would do anything so—so wicked."

"You were quick enough to believe the worst about Grant," Caine pointed out. "You owe him, Juliet. You owe him the chance to clear himself with your sister." His face darkened. "Of course, there's always the risk that Grant won't want Miranda back. I know I wouldn't want a woman who had so little faith in me."

"You don't understand," Juliet cried, quick to leap to her sister's defense. "It was as much a lack of faith in herself that made her believe Grant didn't want her. Randi has always been insecure about herself as an individual. She's always believed that people were only interested in her because she was an identical triplet. She couldn't believe that Grant Saxon—a big, handsome, rich pro football player—would actually want *her!* She thought he merely wanted to be seen with a Post triplet, that any one of us would do."

"I remember Grant telling me about that. It frustrated the hell out of him." Caine flashed a sudden, devilish grin. "That and Miranda's virginity. But he got past both, didn't he? Her lack of self-confidence *and* her virginity."

Juliet blushed scarlet. "I should have known you big-time lady-killers would indulge in locker room—style boasting!"

"No boasting and no locker room, honey. I happened to stop by Grant's house one afternoon and found them—how shall I phrase it?—in a state of dishabille. Your sister was *very* relaxed and *very* content and *very* unvirginal."

Juliet's blush deepened. "Will you kindly shut up?" she said crossly. "Grant had no business telling you Randi was a virgin in the first place."

"He needed to talk to someone about it, and we've always been close. Hey, I've never mentioned it to a soul until now."

"You make it sound like some kind of . . . of

abnormality!" She glowered at him, her tone defensive. "Like some deep, dark family skeleton."

Caine stared at her assessingly, then his eyes suddenly widened with astonished perception. "Good Lord, don't tell me that *you're* one too!"

"That's none of your business, Saxon!"

"You are, aren't you? You're a virgin!"

"It's not a crime. I'm not ashamed to admit it."

"But you're blushing," he pointed out. "Your face is as red as a boiled lobster."

"Your imagery leaves a lot to be desired, Saxon." She crossed her arms over her chest and scowled at him.

"I think in terms of food. I run a restaurant, remember? How about this one? Your cheeks are as red as a ripe persimmon. Pink as a watermelon? Or a cherry—No, I'd better stay away from that one, hadn't I?"

She leaped to her feet. "Saxon!"

He laughed. "You should blush more often, Juliet. It makes your eyes an even deeper, darker blue." He stood up, close to her, and gazed down at her. "You really do have the most vivid blue eyes I've ever seen. Sometimes they look almost violet." He swallowed hard. "Like now."

A sudden, sharp tension stretched between them. For one long moment everything in the background seemed to blur for Juliet as she and Caine stared at each other with an intensity and awareness that seemed to pulse as a tangible force.

No, she thought grimly as she felt the tug of his attraction and fought against it. His powerful frame and rugged good looks exuded a compelling virility that most women would find irresistible, she knew. Had *already* found irresistible, judging by the number of framed photos in the Saxon brothers' restaurant. She had no intention of joining his legion of female admirers. She wasn't about to be the second Post to fall for a Saxon. Look at how disastrously things had turned out for Randi!

Oh, no, Caine warned himself sternly as he struggled against the potent force of Juliet's beauty. She was lovely, slender but with delicate curves accentuating her soft, feminine form. And her eyes . . . A man could lose himself in those big blue-violet eyes of hers. But he wasn't about to become the next Saxon to be tied in knots by a Post. She was a triplet—and a virgin! The combination had proven lethal to his brother's freedom and peace of mind. Caine Saxon was not about to become similarly ensnared!

Juliet was the first to break the charged silence. "If you've said everything you came to say, I suggest you leave, Saxon."

"Scared?" he taunted with a sardonic smile. "You needn't be. I have no interest in uptight little virgins."

"That's good. Because *I* have no interest in aging playboy athletes."

"I'm only thirty-four, for Pete's sake! That's hardly aging! And I'm *not* a playboy!"

"Well, I'm not uptight."

"Okay, okay. Look, Juliet, let's call a truce, shall we? We've both agreed that neither of us is susceptible to each other's . . . er, charms—"

"How true!"

Caine sent her a quelling glance and continued. "But we do share a common goal—to end Miranda and Grant's unhappiness." He heaved a weary sigh. "For our own sakes as much as theirs. I know I can't take much more of Grant's misery. He's carrying a torch as big as China for your sister and I really do. I feel for him. But last night he played 'Send in the Clowns' forty-three times in a row. One day he played it sixty-seven times. I counted," he added glumly.

Juliet couldn't help sympathizing with him.

"Randi has a whole stack of torchy, weepy songs she plays over and over again. Livvy and I call it music-to-commit-suicide-by."

"Things can't go on like this, Juliet. They've got to meet, to talk things over . . ."

"Not if Grant really did spend a weekend in Richmond with Darla Ditmayer. If he did that, Randi's better off with her sad songs than with him."

"But what if Grant and Miranda are the innocent victims of some nasty little scheme of Sophia's?" Caine paused. "What then, Juliet?"

"Then I think we should do everything in our power to straighten things out between them," she said thoughtfully.

He smiled. It was the first genuine smile that Juliet had seen from him, and it had a devastating effect upon her senses. Her stomach lurched and her pulse raced. She seemed to glow inside. It was impossible not to smile back at him.

"That's what I was hoping you'd say," he said huskily. She was smiling at him, a warm, sweet smile, and he felt his breath catch in his chest. His gaze was riveted to her face and he couldn't seem to look away. She was so beautiful—that exquisite bone structure, that flawless complexion, those intriguing eyes. Warning signals went off in his head. He'd never reacted so intensely to a woman's smile!

"I'll talk to Sophia," he said, struggling to sound cool and nonchalant. "I'll let you know what she says."

Juliet nodded. "You know," she said thoughtfully, "even if Sophia did cause the breakup, it's not going to be all that easy to get Grant and Randi back together again."

"I know. They've been apart a whole month, they've gone through the trauma of a canceled wedding—and there's the serious matter of

Miranda's total lack of trust in Grant. It's *not* going to be easy, Juliet, but I think we've got to try."

"If only to avoid listening to 'Send in the Clowns' forty-three more times, hmm?"

He laughed. "Shall we shake on our tentative alliance?"

He held out his hand. Juliet hesitated a moment, then placed her small hand in his big one. With one fluid movement, he pulled her toward him. Still holding her hand, he cupped her chin with his other hand and took her mouth with his.

Juliet was too stunned to protest. She hadn't expected Caine to make that kind of a move. Nor had she expected his hard, sensual mouth to feel so soft and gentle upon hers. For a split second she stood stock still while Caine's lips moved lightly, questioningly over her own. And then, as if of their own volition, her eyelids fluttered shut and her lips parted.

His tongue slipped into her mouth to probe the moist warmth within, and rubbed against her own tongue with a seductive intimacy that made her limbs go weak. A hot swell of excitement rolled through her, and she trembled with awakening urgency.

She was vaguely aware that Caine had dropped his hands to fold her deeply within his embrace. Her body surged against his and a small, soft moan escaped from her throat. Her breasts swelled and her nipples tightened as they pressed against the muscular wall of his chest. His warm hands smoothed over her back, massaging and stroking, sliding around to her sides to tease along her ribs, stopping tantalizingly, maddeningly, at the undersides of her aching breasts.

The kiss deepened, insistent and intimate, and pure, raw pleasure filled her. Her senses were full of Caine, of the taste and feel and scent of him.

Driven by a compulsive need to be even closer, Juliet's arms wound around his neck, and she molded herself to his hard frame.

Her mind was clouded. There was no time to think or reason. She was lost in the cloudy, shadowed world of sensation. When his lips moved to her neck she tilted her head to give him greater access. When his big hands cupped her bottom and lifted her slightly she settled herself snugly into the cradle of his thighs.

"Juliet." He groaned her name. His lips were buried in the silken, scented hollow of her throat. His whole body was taut with an aching urgency that had swept over him, unexpectedly and unconditionally, the moment he'd felt her soft, sweet mouth open under his.

The force of his own desire left him reeling. When was the last time a woman's kiss had so thoroughly shattered his control? Caine Saxon had always been the master of his passions. As an athlete, he had trained his body to obey his mind, and his iron self-control extended to any situation in the physical realm.

But this time the driving need that surged through him was beyond his mind's control. He held her tightly, possessively, as he trailed a path of stinging little kisses along the slender curve of her neck. Her sweetly feminine scent intoxicated him. The feel of her rounded softness pressed hotly against him totally clouded his rational thinking processes.

Juliet felt the urgency within him, felt his hands become more demanding, his caresses more intimate. His breathing was rapid and shallow, as was her own, and his heart was thundering beneath her fingertips. She sensed his control was tentative at best, and a heady power warmed her. He wanted her. He was aching for her, throbbing for her. She could feel the full force of his arousal.

"Juliet, I want you." His voice was hoarse and he clutched her fiercely. "I've never wanted any woman as much as I want you this moment."

His own admission floored him. It was true, but he'd had no intention of telling *her*! The words had simply slipped out, another symptom of his shocking loss of self-control. Caine Saxon was not given to passionate declarations. The fact that he'd made this one alarmed him.

Juliet snuggled closer to him, filled with a sudden surge of tenderness for him. She'd never before inspired such unabashed masculine need. The men she'd known were so calm and controlled. None had ever been swept away with passion, nor had they inspired a similar abandon in her. But Caine . . .

"This is crazy!" he exclaimed. His hands closed around her shoulders and he drew back slightly to look at her. It was a major tactical error, he admitted to himself with a silent groan. She looked incredibly, sensually appealing. Her lips were softly swollen from his kisses, her dark hair was slightly tousled, and her eyes were a deep violet shade. "Juliet, I—I'd—we—" He cleared his throat.

She was looking at him in a way that blotted out his thoughts. "I think I'd better leave now," he finally managed to say. He began to back slowly away from her. Her steady gaze was mesmerizing him. He had to get away before he was totally consumed by her . . . power?

He was afraid of her! Juliet thought. The dawning realization filled her with incredulity—and amusement. But the look on his face, the way he was moving away from her, as if willing her not to drag him back, was unmistakable. Caine Saxon was a full foot taller than she and outweighed her by well over a hundred pounds, but he was afraid of her!

"Caine," she called sweetly, experimenting with

her newly discovered power. She held out her hand to him and watched in fascination as he visibly struggled to resist taking it. He wanted to come back to her. He was waging an internal civil war to stay away from her. The knowledge thrilled her. She felt as irresistible as Delilah, as influential as Eve. He made her feel unique, and as one of three identical sisters, she'd never felt unique in her entire life! She was always part of a matched set.

"I'll talk to Sophia and . . . uh, be in touch," Caine said. He turned and headed for the door. Damn, what was the matter with him? he wondered. *She* was the virgin, but *he* was the one running away in a state of nervous anxiety! Why, he'd faced two-hundred-eighty-pound defensive linemen in his football career and had never felt this urge, this *need* to run.

It was a protective instinct, he consoled himself as he stepped onto the wide front porch. Look what her sister had done to his brother! Grant Saxon had been a cheerful bon vivant who'd been reduced to listening to endless refrains of "Send in the Clowns" after he'd tangled with Miranda Post. And look at the way Bobby Lee Taggert always trailed after Olivia Post. Like a faithful puppy dog!

Caine couldn't fathom himself in either role. He did not carry torches and he was not a tagalong. Those Post triplets were dangerous! A must to avoid. He would do what he could for Grant, but he intended to steer clear of Juliet Post.

"Scared?" A voice asked softly, tauntingly, as he stepped off the porch.

He whirled around to find Juliet standing in the open doorway, watching him.

He managed a choked sound of protest. That the little demon should have guessed what he was feeling! Never had he felt so mortified, so at a loss as a man.

"You needn't be," she went on. "I have no interest in aging playboy athletes, remember?"

"And I have none in violet-eyed virgins who are cloned three times over!"

"Good!" She grinned at him. "Then let's reinstate our truce. After all, neither of us is susceptible to the other's . . . uh, charms."

"How true!" Caine unlocked his car and climbed in. As he pulled away from the curb, he glanced in his rearview mirror. Juliet was still standing on the porch, and he had the uncomfortable feeling that she was laughing at him.

Three

"Julie, it's for you," Olivia called, tucking the telephone receiver in the crook of her neck while she continued to deftly arrange pink and white buttercream roses on the iced chocolate fudge cake.

There was no reason for her heart to begin thumping so violently, Juliet admonished herself as she retrieved the receiver from Olivia. The call could be from anyone. From a potential customer wanting to hire the Post Sisters' Catering Service, from any number of friends, or . . . from Caine Saxon. Her pulses careened wildly.

"Hello?" she said into the phone.

"Is this really Juliet?" It *was* Caine Saxon, and he sounded suspicious. "How do I know it's not Olivia or Miranda pretending to be Juliet? Hell, you all sound exactly alike. Even your voices are cloned!"

"You're paranoid, Saxon. Why would Livvy or Randi pretend to be me? They don't want to talk to you."

At the mention of the name Saxon Olivia mangled a buttercream rose and stared at Juliet with wide blue eyes. Juliet stretched the phone cord as far as she could to slip around the corner and out of sight.

"Hmm, I guess you must be Juliet at that." Caine gave a slight laugh. "The nasty, sharp-tongued one." His voice lowered. "I talked to Sophia today and I'm sorry to say my suspicions were correct. She was the one who left the message on your answering machine and she arranged for her friend to call your sister. She even had Darla Ditmayer ready to say she was in Richmond with Grant, in case Miranda called to inquire."

Juliet gasped. "How could she?" The calculated cruelty of the other woman's acts appalled her. "Why would she do such a thing? And to her own brother!"

"I don't think she expected your sister to break the engagement," Caine said slowly. "But I'm not making any excuses for Sophia and I told her so. I also told our mother what happened and she's as furious and disgusted as I am. We both had a long talk with Sophia." His voice hardened. "My sister is ready to make a full confession—and apology—to both Grant and Miranda."

Juliet guessed that Sophia Saxon had been given little choice in the matter. It must have been a thoroughly unpleasant scene with Caine Saxon letting his sister know the full vent of his fury and disgust. Not that she felt a bit sorry for the scheming Sophia. What misery she had caused both the Posts and the Saxons!

"Mom would like Miranda to come over to her house at seven tonight if it's convenient. Grant will be there too. Do you have a catering job tonight, Juliet? Do you think your sister will come?"

Juliet swallowed. She knew how her sister detested confrontations and scenes, and this one promised to be a dandy. Poor Randi. On the other hand, she deserved an apology from that miserable Sophia Saxon. And Grant would be there. . . .

"We're not working tonight," she said. "And maybe Randi will come—if Livvy and Bobby Lee and I come too."

"A Post never travels without her entourage, eh?"

"One can never be too careful when wandering into Saxon territory," she retorted.

"It seems you have good reason to distrust the Saxons," Caine said soberly. "At least one of them. I'm sorry my sister did this, Juliet. I'm ashamed and appalled and deeply sorry."

She hadn't expected an apology from Caine. It wasn't his fault, after all. She found herself warming to him in spite of herself. He was genuinely concerned about his brother's happiness, and she could certainly relate to that.

"You don't owe anyone an apology, Caine. If it weren't for you, we would never have learned the truth."

Her voice was soft, and he felt his body respond with a growing tautness. He was instantly on his guard. The image of her calling to him, her hand outstretched and beckoning, rushed vividly to mind. He'd wanted to take her hand, to pull her into his arms and kiss her until she was breathless and trembling and clinging. And then . . .

He forced away thoughts of that tantalizing prospect with the same willpower he'd used to keep himself from returning to her arms. He refused to get involved with the sexually inexperienced identical triplet sister of his brother's ex-fiancée! There were enough strings in that one to ensure a hopeless tangle—and he wasn't about to get caught up in it!

"I did what I had to do for Grant," he said

brusquely. "I wouldn't have exposed Sophia for anyone else but him."

"I understand." Empathy surged through her. It would be dreadful to have to admit that your own sister was scheming, jealous, and cruel. But Caine Saxon had faced it and dealt with it. "Thank you, Caine," Juliet said quietly.

Her voice seemed to burn him through the telephone wires. Caine felt the heat surge through his body and was thoroughly alarmed. How could the mere sound of her voice bring forth such a response from him? It was a phenomenon he didn't care to explore.

"Tonight at seven at my mother's house. Make sure Miranda is there," he said gruffly, and quickly hung up.

Juliet came back into the kitchen and replaced the receiver in its cradle. "Saxon?" Olivia said, staring at her. "Was I hearing right?"

"Livvy, did you know how much Sophia Saxon has resented us through the years?" Juliet asked musingly.

"Sophia Saxon? Why, I've never given her much thought. *Has* she resented us?"

Juliet sank into one of the kitchen chairs. "Like you wouldn't believe!"

Miranda cried when her sisters told her of Sophia Saxon's scheming. And then she panicked. "Grant will never forgive me!" she wailed. "I didn't trust him. I broke our engagement without even telling him why!"

"You thought he knew why, Randi," Olivia reminded her in a futile attempt to console her. "You thought he'd spent the weekend in Richmond with Darla. We all did."

"Sophia set it up so we would think exactly that," added Juliet. "You know, I haven't thought of high

school or cheerleading in years, but right now I'm
so glad we took up three places on the squad and
kept Sophia off."

Olivia sniffed. "She wouldn't have made it if we'd
been twins. She did the clumsiest cartwheel I'd
ever seen."

Miranda was not diverted by her sisters' reminis-
cences. "What am I going to say to Grant? I—I still
love him, you know. Even when I thought he'd
cheated on me, I couldn't stop loving him. That's
what's made it so painful, so—so unbearable!"

Olivia took Miranda's hand in hers. "And I'm
sure he still loves you, too, Randi. I think that
everything is going to work out just fine!"

Juliet wished she could share Livvy's optimism,
but right now she felt more aligned with Randi's
pessimism. Would Grant be able to forgive Randi's
total lack of faith? If only she and Livvy had forced
Randi to confront Grant about the alleged weekend
in Richmond! Caine Saxon hadn't hesitated to
confront *his* sister with his suspicions.

But it wasn't all Randi's fault, Juliet thought loyally. Why couldn't Grant Saxon have played a more
active role in seeking the cause of his broken
engagement, rather than passively accepting
Randi's sudden seeming change of heart? Why
hadn't he stormed over here and demanded an
explanation from Randi? Why hadn't he made her
listen to him?

That's what Caine would have done. The
thought came instantly to Juliet's mind, and she
felt her cheeks grow warm. If Caine Saxon wanted
a woman, there was no way he would meekly allow
her to keep him at bay.

What would it be like to be passionately sought
by Caine Saxon? she mused dreamily. Unbidden
came the memories of herself in his arms—of the
strength and seduction of his large hands, of the
exciting warmth of his mouth, the erotic caress of

his tongue. A flash of heat rippled through her. The sensations she'd evoked were so real, she almost expected to find herself back in Caine's arms.

But she was with her sisters in Randi's small bedroom in the little frame house they'd grown up in. Their parents had turned it over to the triplets when they'd retired to Arizona four years before. Sniffling, Randi walked over to her small stereo and put on a stack of records. Olivia and Juliet exchanged glances. More music-to-commit-suicide-by. Juliet thought briefly of Caine and wondered if he was with his brother, listening to yet another replay of "Send in the Clowns."

"Please," Randi whispered as she lay down on her bed. "I want to be alone for a while."

Her sisters tiptoed obligingly from the room.

Randi's pessimism was well founded, Juliet decided grimly as the three sisters filed into Mrs. Saxon's spotlessly tidy living room at five minutes before seven that evening. Bobby Lee had come along for moral support—which, by the looks of things, they were all going to need.

The four Saxons sat on one side of the room, their faces tense and implacable. Juliet scanned them briefly. Mrs. Saxon, a handsome, graying matron somewhere near sixty, had obviously been crying. Her eyes were red-rimmed and she held a handkerchief balled in her fist. Sophia, tall and attractive, sat in a chair and stared at the Posts with cold brown eyes. Sophia wasn't at all sorry she'd caused Randi trouble, Juliet thought indignantly, although she was probably sorry she'd been caught.

"I told you y'all should've dressed alike," Bobby Lee drawled in a whisper. "It would've been like a knife in that viper's gut."

The sisters had chosen not to follow Bobby Lee's method of revenge and had dressed unidentically. Juliet wore canary yellow slacks and a yellow cotton blouse, Olivia wore a similar outfit in bright green, and Miranda wore one in bright blue. All wore earrings and shoes in matching colors.

Juliet's eyes were drawn to Caine. He looked big and masculinely imposing in jeans and a black and gold football jersey. A Pittsburgh Steelers one, of course. Her gaze flicked to Grant Saxon. Surprisingly, Grant was formally dressed in a light gray suit. He resembled his brother, but his features were finer, and his eyes were an ordinary shade of brown, not the unique amber color of Caine's.

The Posts and Bobby Lee sat together on the long sofa on the opposite side of the room from the Saxons. For several moments everyone simply sat and stared at each other in awkward silence.

Sophia was the first to speak, and her voice was cool. Condescending too. "It was helpful of you Posts to come color-coded tonight, but could you let us in on the code? Tell us who is wearing what color?"

To Juliet's surprise, Caine spoke up. He was staring at her intently and his voice was firm as he said, "Juliet is in yellow." He didn't sound as certain when he added, "Miranda is in green and Olivia in blue?"

How had he known her? Juliet wondered. Her eyes were captured by his, and neither seemed able to break the gaze. Her heart began to beat a little faster.

How had he known which one was Juliet? Caine wondered. He was astonished at his own perception. He'd had to guess at the identity of the other two Posts, but he'd known Juliet from the moment his eyes had connected with hers.

"Close, but no cigar, Caine," Bobby Lee said jovially. "Livvy is in green and Randi's wearing blue. But, hey, one out of three isn't—"

"If we can dispense with the triplet jokes," Sophia interrupted, "I'd like to get on with this. I have a date tonight. Grant, Miranda, I apologize." She stood up and swept from the room.

"That's it?" Bobby Lee asked incredulously. "We got all dressed up to come over here and that's all there is to it?"

"Sophia is terribly sorry for what she's done," Mrs. Saxon interjected quickly. "But she does have difficulty in expressing emotion."

"I don't think she's sorry at all," Olivia said darkly.

"Did you expect her to grovel at our feet?" Grant said. He stood up, his face hard. "What she did was reprehensible, but it needn't have been more than a bad joke if Miranda had the necessary faith and trust in me. But, put to the test, she failed miserably in those areas."

Miranda stood up as well. "Grant." She gazed at him, her deep blue eyes pleading. "I—I know it's inadequate, but I'm truly sorry. I made the worst mistake of my whole life by—by believing that ugly story. If you can only forgive me, I promise to—"

"You're right, Miranda. Your apology is inadequate," Grant said coldly.

Juliet watched Randi's face crumple. She sagged against Bobby Lee, who draped a supportive, brotherly arm around her shoulders. Was that a flicker of satisfaction in Grant's eyes? Juliet wondered. It was! An explosion of fireworks seemed to go off in her head.

"While you're on the subject of inadequate apologies, mister," she said, crossing the room to stand directly in front of Grant, "your sister Sophia's apology was far from adequate. It was downright insulting! And if you think you can lay the blame for this entire mess on Randi, you're sorely mistaken. *You* played a role in it yourself, you know! You avoided a confrontation too. You allowed yourself to be fobbed off by Livvy and me over the phone, you sent letters and flowers, but if you hadn't been such a wimp and had come over yourself—"

"Wimp?" roared Grant. His hands closed over Juliet's shoulders and he gave her a shake. "I was devastated—not to mention publicly humiliated—by having my fiancée break our engagement two weeks before the wedding. I tried to be patient with your sister, I tried to be understanding and sensitive, and *you* have the unmitigated gall to call me a wimp?"

"Take your hands off my sister, you big gorilla!" shrieked Miranda, charging across the room to seize Juliet's arm. For one who loathed scenes, Randi was certainly taking an active part in this one, Juliet thought with astonishment.

"Let go of my sister!" Miranda was crying and tugging at Juliet's arm. Grant seemed frozen to the spot. He continued to hold Juliet while he stared wide-eyed at the weeping, tugging Miranda.

Juliet felt like the rope in a tug-of-war. She tried to escape from her position between the warring couple to no avail. Finally, Grant seemed to recover himself. He dropped his hands from her shoulders and grabbed Miranda.

"Miranda, for heaven's sake, get hold of yourself!" he ordered.

"Let me go!" Miranda began to pummel him with her small, clenched fists.

Juliet quickly slipped from between them. She was on her way back to the Posts' side of the room when she was intercepted by Caine. He took her hand and led her into the adjoining dining room.

"Are you all right?" he asked quietly. He smoothed her slightly tousled hair with his long fingers.

Juliet cast a glance into the living room in time to see Miranda break free from Grant's hold and flee to Olivia's comforting arms. Mrs. Saxon was fluttering about, looking extremely distressed. Grant muttered an oath and stormed from the room. They heard the front door slam shut.

"I'm okay," Juliet said glumly. "But Randi isn't. This didn't go at all like we'd planned, did it, Caine? I think things between them are worse than ever."

"It didn't occur to me that Grant would be nursing his wounded pride. With a group present, he naturally tried to get some of his own back." Caine looked thoughtful. "Next time we'll have to get them alone together, with no witnesses present."

"Next time?" Juliet stared at him. "Are you kidding? It's too dangerous! They were almost mauling each other this time!" She was tense with anxiety, and flexed her shoulders and rubbed her neck. "I was between them, remember?"

"Relax, Juliet, you're wound tight as a spring," he said huskily. His fingers tangled with her own as he began to massage the nape of her neck. She cast him a quick, darting glance and was caught by the hunger in his amber eyes. Her own eyes widened and darkened. It was impossible to look away.

He moved his fingers over her nape in a rhythmic caress as their gazes clung. Once again Juliet experienced the odd sensation of having the background and everyone in it fade from view. Once again there was just she and Caine in their own private world.

He was looking at her mouth, and her lips parted in unconscious invitation. As his hot amber gaze lowered, she felt her nipples tingle, as if he had actually touched them. There was a warm heaviness throbbing deep in her abdomen, between her thighs. . . .

Juliet quickly and abruptly pulled away. What was happening to her? She felt weak and soft. Her whole body was aching for the masterful pressure of his. Despite the horrid scene that had just taken place, despite the fact that across the room her sister was sobbing over his brother, that his mother was nervously fluttering about—despite these impossible circumstances, he had made her want him.

His touch, his gaze had blocked out their surroundings, making her aware solely of him and what he was making her feel. What was this awesome power he had over her? She looked up at him, apprehensive and confused.

"I don't understand it either," he said. "But if it's any consolation, you have the same effect on me."

It was disconcerting that he'd read her so clearly. "Whatever do you mean?" she hedged.

"This is certainly the wrong time and the wrong place, but it does raise some interesting possibilities, doesn't it, Juliet?" He flashed a rakish smile that should have irritated her, but that made her smile instead.

"I could make your head spin in bed, Juliet," he said, his voice low. "Are you going to let me?"

She felt the hot color stain her cheeks even as she willed herself not to blush. She heard Caine chuckle softly and eyed him defiantly. "One word about blushing virgins and you've had it, Saxon!"

"Julie," Bobby Lee called, almost pleading. "Let's get out of here!" Juliet turned and saw he had one arm around a weeping Miranda and one around a quietly sniffling Olivia. Mrs. Saxon was hovering.

"I'll call you tomorrow and we can discuss the next strategic move," Caine said softly as she started to walk away.

"In getting me to bed? Forget it, Saxon!" she hissed.

"I was talking about getting Grant and Miranda

back together," he shot back. "You seem quite preoccupied with going to bed with me, Juliet. Not that I'm complaining, mind you."

Juliet laughed. She certainly hadn't meant to, but she couldn't seem to help it. Then she glanced at her sisters and instantly sobered. "Caine, do you think they'll ever get things straightened out between them?"

Sophia Saxon chose that moment to waltz into the living room, "Did Grant leave yet?" she asked her mother.

"No, yes, I don't know." Poor Mrs. Saxon was distraught.

"He has a date tonight," Sophia continued with saccharine sweetness. "With Darla Ditmayer. I do hope he isn't late picking her up."

"Sophia!" Mrs. Saxon exclaimed in horror. Sophia sauntered out of the room.

"We're leaving!" Bobby Lee said decisively as Miranda and Olivia exchanged shocked, tearful glances. "Come on, Julie," he called over his shoulder as he hustled the other two Posts out the front door.

"Juliet, wait!" Caine's voice halted her in her tracks.

She whirled around, her eyes flashing with fury. "I could kill that horrid sister of yours!"

"You'll have to take a number," he said grimly. "Juliet, we can't let another month elapse before we take action. Then it really will be too late for Grant and Miranda."

"I don't want my sister to be hurt any more by your awful brother!"

"He's not awful. This is the first date he's had since Miranda broke up with him. And keep in mind that he didn't know Miranda would be here tonight. We just made the arrangements today, remember?"

"We should have stayed out of it! I *am* staying

out of it from now on. Good-bye, Caine." She rushed from the house.

It was a dreary, silent ride home. When they arrived at the Posts' house, Miranda ran upstairs to her room and closed the door. A few minutes later the sound of heartbreakingly melancholy music drifted down the stairs to where Juliet, Olivia, and Bobby Lee sat glumly in the living room.

"Oh, no!" Bobby Lee groaned. "Not 'It's Over' again! Randi's going to drive herself crazy if she keeps listening to those songs."

"Wouldn't it be ironic if Grant ended up with Darla Ditmayer, after all?" Olivia said gloomily. "Oh, poor Randi! It just isn't fair! She really loves Grant."

"And people in love are sometimes irrational." Bobby Lee frowned. "If only we could do something to get them back together. I think Grant is still in love with Randi too. It's a real shame we were all in that living room tonight. I have a feeling there would've been a different outcome if they'd been alone."

Juliet looked thoughtful. "Do you really think so, Bobby Lee?"

"Sure do, sugar."

When the telephone rang at ten-thirty that night Juliet hurried to answer it, somehow knowing who was calling. Her instincts proved correct.

"I want to speak to Juliet," Caine Saxon said.

Her heart gave an odd little leap. "This is Juliet. Not one of the other ones impersonating her," she added with a smile.

"I'm calling from Grant's house, Juliet." Caine sounded grim. "Earlier tonight I got a call from Carl Watkins, the bartender at the Charade Lounge. Grant was downing double Scotches and in no shape to drive anywhere. He stood Darla Ditmayer up and went out to get loaded. I brought him home and put him to bed. He's up in his room now, listening to 'Send in the Clowns.' "

"Ohh!" Juliet groaned.

"I think he's starting to lose it, Juliet. He's in terrible shape. How's Miranda?"

"In the same miserable shape, I'm afraid. It's affecting all of us, Caine. Even Bobby Lee is starting to get morose, and he's always been the jolliest person imaginable."

"Juliet, I have a plan, which I hope will have a better outcome than tonight's debacle. Are you interested?"

"I'll do anything if it means making Randi happy again," Juliet said fervently.

"Good. I thought we'd arrange a meeting between them at the Apple Country Inn out on Route 250. Do you know the place? It's very romantic, very secluded—and there are rooms available if one wishes to . . . er, prolong the evening till the next morning."

"You'd know all about such arrangements, wouldn't you?" Juliet was appalled to hear herself say that. Good heavens, she sounded almost . . . jealous! she thought. Nothing could be further from the truth, she quickly assured herself.

Caine chuckled. "Let's deal with Grant and Miranda first, Juliet. Then we'll move on to the infinitely more interesting subject of us."

"There is no 'us,' Saxon!" She was thankful that she was sitting alone in the darkness and no one, not even she herself, could see how flushed she was.

"Do you agree with my choice of locale?" he asked. "In such a setting, with such opportunities available, how can they miss?"

"I think you're being overly optimistic, Saxon,"

she said dampeningly. "Our first goal should be to get them to say a civil word to each other."

He ignored her comment. "I'll make dinner reservations for eight tomorrow night. Now, how do we get them there without either becoming aware of our little scheme?"

"I could ask Randi to drive out to ask the chef for a recipe," Juliet suggested. "We sometimes do ask various restaurants if they'll share recipes with us to use in our business."

"Their cold strawberry soup is delicious," Caine said. "Tell her to ask for that recipe."

"Strawberry soup?" She made a face. "It sounds positively poisonous!"

"Someday I'll take you to the Apple Country Inn and buy you a bowl. After your sister and my brother are safely reunited."

"Forget it! When I go to dinner I make it a point to be home well in time for breakfast the next morning."

"There you go again, talking about going to bed with me. I merely invited you for a bowl of soup, my sweet. You do have a one-track mind, don't you?"

"Stop it, Saxon!"

He laughed, a husky, sexy laugh that sent a sensual quiver along her spine.

"How are you going to get Grant to the inn?" she asked in a desperate attempt to change the subject.

Thankfully, Caine allowed the change of topic. "Maybe I could use the same line about the strawberry soup recipe. I could say that I felt The Knight Out absolutely has to have it on our menu and that the chef will only give it out in person. Grant is so out of it these days, I don't think he'll even question it."

"I don't think Randi will, either."

"Good. Then it's set for eight o'clock tomorrow.

Shall we unobtrusively make an appearance at the inn to see how it goes between them?"

She would be dying of curiosity—and anxiety, Juliet acknowledged to herself. And if things went wrong, Randi might need her. "Maybe I will go," she said slowly.

"It's very important that we stay out of sight. I'll pick you up tomorrow at seven-fifteen."

She really should drive out herself, she thought. There was no need to go with Caine Saxon. "All right. Seven-fifteen." She bit her lip in vexation. Why on earth had she said *that*? She quickly reversed herself. "Never mind, I'll drive myself."

"You *are* scared, aren't you, honey?"

"Of you? I most certainly am not!"

"Maybe you're afraid of the way I make you feel." That laugh again, that low laugh that made her tingle with a primitive sexual excitement. "It's quite normal, you know. Women are often afraid of the men that they're powerfully attracted to. I'm told that virgins are apt to be especially antagonistic."

"And from where do you draw your facts?" she demanded hotly. Her whole body was one heated blush. She refused to admit it, but his suggestive supposition actually made sense to her in an odd sort of way.

"I made them up," he replied cheerfully.

"Oh! You!" Juliet glared at the phone as if it were to blame for her discomfiture. "You're—You're—" Why did she have to become incoherent at a time like this? No doubt the cleverly scathing retort she longed to throw at him would occur to her a few hours from now.

"I'm going to pick you up at seven-fifteen tomorrow, partner," Caine finished calmly. "Juliet?"

"What?"

"It may interest you to know that Sophia never made her date tonight." There was a particular satisfaction in Caine's tone. "I intercepted the guy as he pulled into the driveway. Told him that Sophia must have gotten her dates mixed up, that she'd already left with another man. He drove off in a huff."

"You really told him that?" Juliet exclaimed, instantly diverted by the tale.

"I felt I owed it to Grant—and to Miranda. And that's just what I told Sophia."

"I bet she turned purple!" Juliet said gleefully.

"A ferocious shade of mauve. Good night, sweet Juliet, my fair accomplice."

She smiled. "Good night, Caine Saxon."

Four

What did one wear on a sisterly surveillance mission? Juliet wondered as she looked over the contents of her wardrobe a half hour before Caine was due to arrive. One would naturally dress up a bit to go to dinner at the Apple Country Inn, but was this an actual dinner date? Caine had offered to buy her a bowl of strawberry soup at some unspecified future date, but he hadn't mentioned dinner tonight.

Juliet pondered the question before finally selecting a silky royal blue dress with a jewel neck, dolman sleeves, and full skirt. It must be a dinner date, she decided. Unless Caine planned for them to lurk outside and spy on Grant and Miranda through a window. She glanced out her own window at the rain pouring down. No, they wouldn't be lurking outside in this weather. The sky was already dark and the rain showed no signs of abating. The National Weather Service had predicted severe thunderstorms for tonight. It wasn't the best weather for a romantic evening, Juliet thought with a frown. Not that *she* was planning to indulge in one, of course, but Randi and Grant needed all the help they could get.

With a small sigh, Juliet slipped into a pair of high-heeled black pumps and affixed dangling blue and silver earrings to her earlobes before starting to apply her makeup.

"Julie?" Olivia burst into the room, carrying a saucepan and a spoon. "Taste this. What's it missing?"

Juliet sampled a spoonful of the thick, green, pasty looking liquid.

"What's it supposed to be?"

"Cream of artichoke and avocado soup. I'm kind of making it up as I go along. I thought it might be an interestingly different appetizer to serve at the Friends of Mr. Jefferson Lawn and Garden Club luncheon. What do you think?"

"I think this is *too* interestingly different, Livvy." Juliet handed her sister the spoon.

"It's that awful, huh? Should I throw the whole batch away?"

Juliet grinned. "Unless you can get Bobby Lee to eat it."

A bolt of lightning flashed in the sky and both sisters went to the window to stare at the rain. It seemed to be getting heavier. A sharp crack of thunder sounded in the distance.

"I'm worried about Randi driving into the mountains in this rain," Olivia said, frowning. "I wish the Apple Country Inn wasn't so far out on 250. . . ." Her voice trailed off as she continued to watch the rain.

"If Randi doesn't feel like driving up there tonight, we can always reschedule the reconciliation," Juliet said. "Do you think she suspected anything when we sent her on those errands tonight?" They'd had to come up with a reason to get Randi out of the house before Caine arrived at seven-fifteen, and had concocted a list of errands, culminating in the trip to the Apple Country Inn.

"She was too preoccupied to suspect a thing." Olivia sighed. "Poor Randi. Oh, I hope it works out for her and Grant tonight."

"Me too."

"Julie, what about you and Caine Saxon?"

Juliet's cheeks pinked. "He's as concerned about Grant as we are about Randi, Livvy."

Olivia raised her brows. "I see. And that's all there is between you? This mutual concern for his brother and our sister?"

Juliet avoided her sister's eyes. "Uh-huh."

Olivia laughed. "If you say so, Julie. But you look absolutely terrific tonight and I think you're going to bowl Caine Saxon over."

"There have been so many women in his life, Livvy. You've seen the pictures on the walls of The Knight Out. Beauty-contest winners, actresses, models. There's no way *I* could bowl him over." Juliet's voice was unconsciously wistful, and Olivia stared at her sister.

"Julie, Bobby Lee thinks that Caine Saxon is trying to get you into bed."

"We've all read about Charlottesville's famous, professional-league lover boy, Livvy. Caine Saxon tries to get every woman he meets into bed. He isn't going to succeed with me," she said succinctly.

Olivia's blue eyes sparkled. "Bobby told me to tell you to hold out for a ring. Like Randi and I did."

"Tell Bobby Lee that he's becoming as fiendishly scheming as Sophia Saxon!" Juliet picked up the small stuffed Siamese cat that sat on her dresser and threw it at her sister. Olivia ducked, and the cat hit the wall and landed upside down on a chair.

"*I* feel as fiendishly scheming as Sophia Saxon myself," Olivia said with a sudden frown. "Making up that list of errands for Randi, sending her out to a remote country inn in the middle of a terrible storm. Do you really think we're doing the right thing, Julie?"

Juliet sighed. "I hope so, Livvy. We'll know tonight, I suppose."

There was a sudden, hard rap at the front door. "Caine!" Juliet's stomach lurched as her heart did a triple somersault in her chest. She forced herself to take a deep, calming breath. "Livvy, will you answer the door?" She needed another few minutes to compose herself.

"While you pull yourself together?" Olivia cast her sister a knowing look.

Juliet smiled sheepishly. It was difficult, if not impossible, for any of the triplets to hide their emotions from the others. They'd been too close for too long.

Juliet waited at the top of the stairs as Olivia opened the door to Caine. "Hi, Caine!" Olivia greeted him cheerfully.

"Hi, uh . . ." Caine hesitated, and Juliet smiled to herself. Caine didn't know which sister Olivia was. That unnerved him, she knew. Her smile broadened as she remembered his indignant diatribe the time she'd pretended to be Miranda. Caine Saxon liked to keep the players straight on his game card.

Bolstered by her amusement, she started down the steps. And halted midway to stare at Caine. He was wearing jeans, sneakers, and a gray hooded sweat shirt, she saw in dismay. He must have planned to lurk, after all! And she was dreadfully overdressed for it.

Caine was staring at Olivia, who was wearing jeans and a pink and white striped sweater. Juliet's mind went into overdrive. She didn't want Caine to think that she'd dressed up for him, that she'd thought this was a real dinner date, their first date. Never mind that she had. She didn't want *him* to know it!

"Sissy," she called to Olivia, using the childhood name the three sisters had used interchangeably among themselves. Olivia looked up at her in surprise. They hadn't used the old nickname in years. "I need you upstairs for a minute," Juliet continued. She could quickly change into Livvy's jeans and sweater and come back down and Caine would never know the difference. He would think it had been Olivia on the stairs in the blue dress.

Before Olivia could move Caine walked to the foot of the staircase and peered up at Juliet. Their eyes met for just a moment before Juliet quickly looked away. Caine started up the stairs, his amber eyes never leaving her. "Hello, Juliet."

He knew her! Juliet's heart turned over in her chest. No one but their parents and Bobby Lee Taggert and Grant Saxon had ever learned—or bothered to learn—to tell the triplets apart. But Caine Saxon had correctly identified her twice.

"You look beautiful tonight," he said huskily. His warm gaze seemed to caress her, and Juliet allowed herself to bask in that warmth until the thrill of his recognition was replaced by the realization that he knew she'd taken special care to dress just for him.

She flushed, and glanced down at her dress and his jeans, and then caught Livvy's eye.

There were times when the triplets were so attuned to each other that an unspoken communication existed between them. This moment was such a time.

"Julie is dressed up because she has a date later tonight," Olivia said, her eyes meeting Juliet's. The message had been received and acted upon. "As soon as she gets back from this . . . er, spying expedition of yours."

"A date?" Caine frowned. He tore his gaze from Juliet, startled by the sudden vehemence that surged through him. He hated the idea of Juliet with another man, and the fact that he did alarmed him. He had never been the jealous type. And these primitive, possessive feelings surging through him were new to him too.

"With who?" he heard himself ask.

"I'm sure you don't know him," Juliet interjected quickly.

"Mark Walsh, one of our neighbors, an assistant math professor at the university," Olivia said. She smiled, quite pleased with her inventiveness.

Caine frowned. "That name sounds familiar. . . ."

"Livvy, don't you have some cream of artichoke and avocado soup to make?" Juliet prompted. The sooner they dropped the subject of her mythical date, the better.

"Oh! Yes, I guess I do." Olivia drifted off, with a final glance at her sister.

"So who is this jerk you dressed up for?" Caine asked with a scowl. "When did you make this date? I don't know when we'll be back, you know."

Juliet's gaze flickered over him. "We won't be gone long. You obviously plan to sit in the car outside the Inn for a few minutes and then leave." She could tell by the way he'd dressed that he had planned to do just that. And she'd been foolish enough to dress up, as if this were an actual date! She flinched inwardly. Bless Livvy for coming up with that inspired notion of a later date.

"But I thought we'd go out for a drink afterward," Caine said. He did not look pleased.

There was a flash of lightning, instantaneously accompanied by a loud clap of thunder. "We'd better leave before the storm gets any worse," Juliet suggested. They stepped out onto the front porch and she opened her umbrella. A sudden gust of wind swirled the raindrops around them.

"Don't you have an umbrella?" she asked.

"No, I don't."

"Let me guess. Real men don't carry umbrellas?

It's so much more macho to get soaked, I suppose." She watched the relentless downpour of rain. "It's coming down in buckets. Would your machismo be greatly offended if I offered to share my umbrella with you?"

Caine stared at the driving rain. "I gratefully accept your kind offer, Juliet." He scooped her up in his arms and held her high against his chest. "You can hold it above both of us."

They were pelted by cold raindrops as Caine dashed to the car, but Juliet was suddenly impervious to the weather. Instead, she was breathtakingly aware of the strength in the arms that held her, of the hard breadth of his chest. They paused beside the car door, and she looked up to find him staring down at her.

Caine peered into the depths of her violet-blue eyes and felt the searing effect of her gaze flash through him. His mouth lowered slowly to hers, even as he silently protested to himself. It was absurd to want to kiss a woman while standing under an umbrella in the middle of a thunderstorm, but he couldn't stop himself.

"How did you know that it wasn't me who opened the door tonight?" she asked shakily. Her pulses were racing. She needed to put a brake on this crazy excitement he so effortlessly evoked in her and she sought to do so with conversation. "How did you know that it was me on the stairs?"

"No woman looks at me the way you do, Juliet." His face was close to hers and he continued to gaze into her soft blue eyes. "I don't think any woman ever has."

Juliet watched his head descend with a kind of fated submission. You shouldn't let him kiss you, her mind tried to insist. You don't want him to kiss you. But she didn't say a word.

His mouth brushed hers as her hand compulsively sought his face. Her fingertips traced his high cheekbones and the strong curve of his jaw while his lips nibbled softly at hers. And then, suddenly, it wasn't enough. She began to ache for something harder, something more demanding than those teasing, torturous little kisses.

"Caine." She whispered his name against his lips and tangled her fingers in his dark hair.

"What do you want, little rain witch?" His voice was thick with desire, sensuous with triumph. He decided that she had cast a spell over him, and it no longer seemed absurd to be kissing in the rain. But her spell had rebounded—he knew she wanted him as much as he wanted her, and the realization was enormously pleasing.

"I want you to kiss me . . . hard," she said, her eyes dark with hunger.

"Oh, Juliet," he said, his voice raspy. "You'd better watch what you ask for or—"

"I may get it?" Juliet finished enticingly. "Oh, Caine, I hope so!"

She clutched his head and held it to hers, opening her mouth under his, tempting, teasing, deepening the kiss with an ardent expertise she had never dreamed she possessed. She was dizzy with excitement, out of her head with the passion flaring between them in this dark, rainswept night.

"I beg your pardon," a voice intruded, "but unless you're conducting some kind of experiment by using yourselves as a lightning rod, I would advise you both to get in out of the rain."

Caine lifted his head at the sound of the flat, slightly nasal voice. Juliet stared dazedly at the man who stood beside them, clutching a black umbrella. He was at least six or seven inches shorter than Caine.

"Mark!" she gasped, half wondering if he were an apparition. She was still somewhat lost in the hazy throes of passion. "Wh—what are *you* doing here?"

"I'm on my way to your house to borrow some olive oil." Mark adjusted his glasses with one hand and his umbrella with the other. "Sherry needs it for the lasagna she's making for dinner tonight," he added rather proudly.

"Go on in, Mark," Juliet said. "Livvy's there, she'll give it to you."

Mark beamed. "Thanks, neighbor! And . . . er, seriously, you shouldn't be standing out here with all this lightning. There's been a tornado watch issued for Albemarle and Fluvanna counties until midnight tonight."

"He's right, of course," Caine said, his voice still husky with unslaked desire. The sound of it sent sensuous shivers along Juliet's every nerve ending. He opened the car door and set her in the front bucket seat, then raced around the car to join her inside.

They rode in silence to the Charlottesville city limits. Juliet was thoroughly disconcerted by their passionate interlude in the rain. Once again she'd lost all control, all sense of timing and place, when Caine had taken her into his arms. *I could make your head spin in bed, Juliet.* The words he'd spoken yesterday echoed softly, tauntingly in her brain. He could make her head spin *anywhere*, she acknowledged nervously.

She cast a covert glance at him. What was he thinking? That she was hot and hungry for him? She feared he had good reason to think just that. Any woman who went wild in the middle of a tornado watch could certainly be considered an easy score.

And Caine Saxon kept score! His scoreboard was the wall of his restaurant, where his conquests were framed and hung. He'd carried the notion of notches on the bedpost to new heights! Not her, Juliet promised herself. *She* was not joining that rogue's gallery. She'd always been one of a crowd, but—

"Now I remember!"

Caine's exclamation cut in on her reverie.

He was smiling broadly. "Mark Walsh! He's your neighbor, the one you introduced to Sherry Carson, Channel 42's weather girl. And he has a date with Sherry tonight. He's borrowing olive oil for the lasagna she's cooking for him."

"It sounds promising," Juliet said thoughtfully. "I hope so. Mark is such a nice man, but he's very shy. I know he's been lonely."

"Nice, shy, lonely guy, huh? With *two* dates for tonight?"

"What do you mean?" And then she remembered. Olivia had told Caine that Juliet had a date with Mark Walsh tonight.

Caine remembered too. "Why did your sister tell me you had a date with Walsh tonight?"

"She was trying to be fiendishly scheming, like *your* sister," Juliet retorted.

"Uh-oh, I recognize a defensive play when I see one. I'm throwing down the penalty flag, honey. No personal fouls allowed."

"Will you kindly translate? I've made it a point to know as little about football as possible."

"You'll love the game after I've explained it to you. Now, leaving both of our sisters out of it, what's this about a date with Walsh tonight?"

Juliet decided the safest answer was no answer at all. She folded her arms across her chest and stared at the rain pounding at the windshield. The trees along the darkened mountainside were half bent from the force of the wind. "Quite a storm we're having, isn't it?" she said blandly.

"I think I'm beginning to get the drift, Juliet. *I'm* the jerk you dressed up for tonight, aren't I? And when I showed up in jeans, you—"

"You're a jerk, all right," she interrupted dryly.

He didn't take offense. He laughed instead. "Yeah, maybe I am at that. I should've asked you to have dinner with me at the inn tonight. You were expecting me to, weren't you?"

"No, I always dress up to sit in a car outside a restaurant."

"I'm sorry, honey. I'm not dressed for dinner at the inn, but we can—"

"Caine, look!" Juliet interrupted, pointing at the sky. "A bolt of lightning struck that tree down on the hillside! I saw it! It split it right in two!" Actually, she was grateful for the diversion. She didn't want to talk about her expectations for tonight. Or Caine's either!

He shook his head. "We picked one helluva night to stage a reconciliation. Are you afraid of storms, Juliet?"

"No, I like them. I think they're exciting."

He smiled. "I should have known a woman as passionate as you would—"

"But I'm not crazy about being in the mountains in a storm," she added hastily. "We've been driving for a long time." She decided a change of subject was definitely in order. "Are we getting close to the inn?"

"We'll be there soon. Damn! That idiot coming toward us should dim his headlights! They're practically blinding me!"

The car roared past them. Less than two minutes later a van came barreling down the mountainous road in the opposite lane, its headlights glaring. "Every fool in the world is out on the road tonight!" Caine said with disgust. "That van—"

"Was our van!" Juliet sat up straight in her seat. "I'm sure it was, Caine! That means Randi has left the inn."

"It couldn't be," Caine argued. "It's only a few

minutes past eight. They would have hardly had time to say hello."

"If they even said hello. Maybe they took one look at each other and said 'drop dead' instead," Juliet said glumly. "Did the first car that passed us look like Grant's car? He drives a Lambourghini, doesn't he?"

"I couldn't tell what it was. It was too dark. Just as it was too dark for you to be sure that was your van. Don't be so pessimistic, Juliet."

They reached the Apple Country Inn a few minutes later. The two-story frame building seemed to be set in the middle of a sea of mud.

"I'll carry you in," Caine told Juliet, and she did not demur. The mud was so deep and thick, she knew even a short trek through it would spell doom for her new shoes.

To Juliet's surprise, the inn's small dining room was full, every table but one occupied by guests. She scanned the cozy room, staring at each diner, and then repeated the process. Grant and Randi were not seated at any of the tables. "Maybe they already went upstairs," Caine said before she could comment on their very conspicuous absence. "I reserved a room for them."

"You're an eternal optimist." She shook her head. "They're not here, Caine. We passed them on the road."

He set his jaw stubbornly. "I'll ask the proprietor if they've arrived yet."

Five

Caine gave Juliet a thumbs-down sign after his brief chat with Mrs. Castle, the owner and hostess of the inn. "Miranda and Grant *were* here." He heaved a sigh. "Mrs. Castle said a man and a woman fitting their description met in the vestibule, quarreled for a few minutes, and then stormed out. No pun intended," he added as lightning flashed outside the window.

Juliet sighed too. "Now what?"

"We could follow them, I suppose, and spend a miserable evening watching them feel miserable." He brightened. "Or we could stay here and have dinner. Mrs. Castle said the inn's dress code is abolished during bad weather."

"Did she really say that?" Juliet asked doubtfully.

"Scout's honor."

"*You* were a boy scout?"

"An eagle scout. Didn't you know?"

She shook her head, and Caine flashed a sheepish grin. "Sometimes I forget that you aren't well-versed in Saxon history." His grin turned decidedly rakish. "Lots of women are, you know."

"I'm sure. No doubt they have to take a course in it before they're framed and mounted on your wall."

He stared at her quizzically for a moment. "Are you referring to the photographs in the restaurant?" he asked. "You don't think Grant and I had affairs with all the women in those pictures, do you?"

Juliet shrugged and said nothing. A pang of pure jealousy surged through her at the thought of Caine with all those glamorous beauties.

"Good grief, you do!" He gave a short laugh. "Honey, I hate to shatter your illusions, but not even Superman could have made it with all those women and played professional football too."

"You didn't play football all year long," she retorted.

"True. But I did work during the off-season. I was a color commentator for the Pittsburgh Pirates on a local TV station there. That kept me fairly busy."

"But the Pirates are a baseball team, I think," she added uncertainly.

"They are. I happen to be as familiar with baseball as I am with football. I played both all through high school and college, and had a hard time choosing between them when it came time to turn pro."

"More Saxon history, hmm?"

"Pay attention. You're going to be tested on it at the end of the evening." He smiled at her. "Will you have dinner with me, Juliet? There is one table available and it's already reserved for a Saxon and a Post."

She *was* hungry. And she was dressed for the luxuriously appointed dining room, even if he wasn't. "Since the table is reserved for a Saxon and a Post, it might as well be us," she conceded.

"And am I forgiven?"

She stared at him. "Forgiven? For what?"

"For not asking you to dinner in the first place. I should have, of course, but—"

"You were under no obligation to ask me to dinner," she interrupted coolly. "And you still—"

"As I was saying." It was Caine's turn to interrupt, and his voice was just as cool as hers. "I should have asked you to dinner, but I was determined to keep my distance and not become involved with you."

Juliet was totally nonplussed. How was she supposed to reply to *that*? "Well," she began cautiously, "I certainly don't . . ."

"But so much for my determination. We're already deep into the second quarter, aren't we?"

"Do you always talk in incomprehensible football metaphors?" she asked shakily. The way he was looking at her made her feel weak. She quickly turned to follow the bustling Mrs. Castle to their table, a cozy corner one on the far side of the room.

Caine followed closely behind her, laying his big hands on her shoulders as they walked. "Did I tell you how beautiful you look tonight, Juliet?" She was stiff with tension, and his strong fingers began a gentle massage. "When I saw you in that dress, I—"

"Yes, you—you told me," she replied quickly. She took a deep breath. "Caine, tonight we're simply using Randi and Grant's dinner reservation. You don't have to go through your standard dating banter with me."

"I don't use some kind of preplanned, standard banter on my dates!" he protested. "And you do look beautiful." He drew out the chair for her and seated her on it, hovering over her for an extra moment to lightly brush his lips against her glossy dark hair. "You wanted to dress up for me tonight, didn't you, Juliet? You wanted to knock my eyes out."

His perception—and his frankness—made her blush. She shifted away from him and immediately began a thorough study of the menu.

Caine sat down opposite her at the small table. "Juliet." He reached across the table and took her hand in his. Automatically, her eyes lifted. He was staring at her face, which was illuminated by the flickering candlelight. "You succeeded admirably. I'm dazzled."

No man had ever confessed to being dazzled by her, she thought. Wholesome girl-next-door types like her and her sisters seldom inspired such responses. For a moment Juliet felt as alluring and glamorous as one of those bona-fide beauties whose pictures hung on Caine's restaurant wall. And then she remembered that Caine Saxon undoubtedly had more lines than a fisherman and that she was not about to be caught with one.

She carefully withdrew her hand from his. "Everything on the menu looks delicious." She spoke in the polite, impersonal tone one would use in talking to a stranger in a bank line. "What do you recommend?"

"I recommend that you forget about my past and those pictures on the wall. I'm here with you tonight, Juliet."

Her heart jumped, but she ignored his comment. "I think I'll try the chicken pot pie. I've never had it homemade, only the commercially frozen type."

Caine sighed. "Okay, we'll play it your way. This is our first date. We know nothing about one another and we have to make polite small talk over the menu. My, doesn't the sherry tomato bisque *soup* sound interesting? I wonder if they serve it with crackers."

Juliet did not react to his sarcasm. Instead, she

chose to answer him seriously. "I don't know. Perhaps you could request them. And the sherry tomato bisque *does* sound interesting. I think I'll order it myself."

Surprisingly enough, their superficial discussion of the inn's menu led to a more natural conversation about their own respective businesses.

"My sisters and I always loved to cook," Juliet found herself confiding in response to his question of how and why the Posts had begun their catering business. "After we graduated from college with liberal arts degrees and no marketable skills, cooking seemed to be our strongest talent. We thought of opening our own restaurant, but we didn't have the necessary capital. It was Mark Walsh, our next-door neighbor, who suggested catering out of our house. Our folks were retiring and moving to Arizona, so they left us the house and we started cooking."

She smiled in reminiscence. "Our first customers were the Friends of Mr. Jefferson Lawn and Garden Club. They hired us to do their annual luncheon. It was held in one of the ladies' homes and was a huge success. We do the luncheon every year now. It's sort of an anniversary for us."

"Funny how you always remember your first customers. The first people to set foot in our restaurant were a group of fraternity boys, football players on the university team. Grant and I talked to them for hours! Which was fine, since very few others showed up that day."

"Business certainly has picked up for you since then," Juliet said. "I hear you have overflow crowds almost every night."

"The restaurant has been an amazing success." Caine shrugged and smiled. "Oddly enough, we never intended it to turn into a gold mine. Grant and I could both live comfortably on our various investments, but we wanted to do something after retiring from the pros, and opening a restaurant in our old hometown seemed like a good idea. Since it's been so successful we've hired a restaurant-management-school graduate and really aren't too involved in the day-to-day operations anymore."

"It sounds like you Saxons have the golden touch. Everything you do turns out well."

"We used to call it the 'Saxon touch.' And you're right, it seemed like we would actually have to work at failing. Good things just seemed to happen naturally to my brother and me—the big pro football contracts, the product endorsements, the commercials." He paused and frowned. "And then Grant's luck seemed to run out. He was dumped by his fiancée two weeks before his wedding without even being given a reason."

"Randi was terribly hurt by it all too," Juliet said, compelled to defend her sister. "Aside from the usual adolescent crushes, Grant was her first real love—her first lover!"

"And is Bobby Lee Taggert Olivia's first real love and first lover?" Caine asked thoughtfully.

Juliet nodded.

"And you're still a virgin, waiting for that first real love to come along and be your first lover. And when he does you'll undoubtedly marry him."

"There's nothing wrong with that," she said defensively. "It doesn't make me some sort of a freak."

"No." He shook his head. "But it *is* unusual. Why would three beautiful sisters reach the age of twenty-six before two of them finally made love? Why is the third one still holding out? You and your sisters weren't recluses. All three of you have dated through the years. In fact, I distinctly recall Sophia frothing at the mouth your senior year in high school because the Post triplets took up three of the nominations for prom queen. If you'd been elected triple queens, I think she would have slashed her wrists," he added dryly.

"Bonnie Jo Webster was prom queen," Juliet remembered with a smile. "She married her high-school boyfriend and moved to Lynchburg. They have three children now. The oldest girl, Kyla, is—"

"Do you have the answers to my questions, Juliet?" Caine interrupted softly. "Or are you trying to avoid answering them?"

She stared into the candle flame. His questions. Sometimes she'd asked them of herself. "I guess my sisters and I never felt the need, the urge, to be that close to anyone else," she said slowly. "It's hard to put into words. I—I've never tried to explain it to anyone before. . . ."

"Explain it to me, Juliet," Caine demanded quietly.

Their eyes met and clung for a timeless moment. Juliet felt herself being drawn into the mysterious amber depths of his gaze. She was suddenly quite breathless from the intensity of his searching stare.

It required considerable effort to drag her gaze from his, but she mustered her strength and looked away. "From what I've heard—and read," she said, "falling in love involves a certain depend-ency and loss of autonomy. For a while, in the early stages of a passionate relationship, the couple's identities sort of merge." She glanced up at him for confirmation.

He was watching her closely, his expression enigmatic. "Go on."

"Well, I think that's why my sisters and I avoided that kind of intense relationship when we were younger. It took us years to feel like three separate people because we were never treated as individu-als. We were always the triplets, a single entity, a single identity. So none of us was particularly eager to merge herself with another person." She smiled slightly. "You're not following me, are you? I told you it was hard to explain."

"I'm following you very well, Juliet. And I believe I understand why Miranda was so quick to break her engagement to Grant. I think she was still unsure of committing herself."

Juliet considered his theory. "That may be true. It's not easy to give up your identity after finally finding it. For years the boundaries between the three of us were blurred. If one of us wanted to go somewhere, we all felt like we had to go. If one of us liked or disliked something, the other two thought we did too. We even had one name we used interchangeably between us."

"Sissy," he guessed.

She nodded as she fidgeted nervously with a spoon. She had never spoken so frankly about the difficulties of being an identical triplet. She drew in a deep breath. "It took us a long time to grow up and finally learn who we were. I don't think any of us was ready for a mature relationship with a man . . ."

"Until this year," Caine finished for her.

"Yes. Livvy started going with Bobby Lee, and just three months later Randi met Grant. They were serious about each other almost immediately."

"And Juliet has yet to take the plunge." He studied her across the table. Those big, beautiful periwinkle blue eyes of hers were troubled. He saw the traces of uncertainty and confusion in them, and was inexplicably touched.

"I don't want to sound as if I've ever resented Livvy and Randi or being born a triplet," Juliet hastened to add. "I haven't." It was so strange putting her previously unspoken thoughts into words, and she suddenly felt terribly disloyal to her sisters. Why was she talking this way? And to Caine Saxon, of all people!

"My sisters are my best friends. We have wonder-

ful times together. We love each other very much."
All the words ran together and she looked at Caine
worriedly. "The bond between us is incredibly
strong. I don't want you to think that I—that
we . . ."

"Juliet." He leaned across the table and took her
hand. "I understand." He did, too, he realized.
Somehow he understood her with a clarity that
startled him.

A wave of tenderness surged through him. He
felt protective and possessive and . . . oddly fatalis-
tic. Waterloo, he thought. Napoleon met his des-
tiny on the fields of Belgium. His was sitting across
from him in the Apple Country Inn just outside
Charlottesville, Virginia. Strangely enough, the
thought made him smile.

They had almost finished dessert—apple brown
Betty with whipped cream—when a loud crack of
thunder was followed by an earsplitting crash. Several diners rose from their chairs and went to the
windows to peer out, but it was too dark for anything to be seen.

Mrs. Castle hurried into the dining room ten
minutes later. "One of the giant pin oaks was
struck by lightning about a quarter of a mile down
the road," she announced to the diners. "It's lying
across the road and has blocked it completely."

"In which direction?" a man called out. "Toward
Charlottesville or Waynesboro?"

"Charlottesville," said Mrs. Castle. "We've called
the state police to report it, but they don't think a
road crew can get here tonight to clear it." She
smiled. "Fortunately, nobody here will be affected.
Everyone has room reservations for the night, and
we'll do our best to keep you comfortable until the
road is cleared sometime tomorrow."

Juliet stared at the woman, as thunderstruck as
the unfortunate pin oak. Her gaze flew to Caine's

face. "I can't spend the night here!" she said breathlessly. "I have to go home!"

Caine's expression was strangely resigned. He wondered why the news of the blocked road didn't surprise him. Somehow it seemed almost prophetic that he and Juliet would be spending the night together here. And that they would move firmly and irrevocably into the third quarter. He didn't dare quote another football metaphor to her, though, he decided as he studied her face. Her eyes were wide with apprehension and her hand was shaking as she replaced her coffee cup in its saucer.

"Caine, we're not staying here!" Juliet fought to suppress the panic rising within her.

"Honey, I don't think we have much of a choice," he replied calmly. "Not if there's a tree blocking the road."

"You can drive over the branches, can't you?"

"Drive over a giant pin oak? Are you kidding? I have a Ferrari, Juliet, not a bulldozer."

"There *must* be a way to get back to Charlottesville," she insisted. "Maybe we can drive around the tree, alongside the road."

"There are woods on either side of the road," he reminded her. "Thick, dense, uncut woods. And if you think I'm going to even attempt to drive my car through a mountain forest—in the middle of a severe storm yet!—you're out of your sweet little mind."

Mrs. Castle came over to their table. "Is everything all right?" she asked solicitously. She was going from table to table, reassuring the guests.

Who didn't seem to need reassurance at all, Juliet thought as she glanced around the dining room. Nobody seemed upset or anxious about being trapped here, nobody but herself. Because all the others were travelers or lovers who'd planned to spend the night here all along.

"Is the road really impassable?" she asked the older woman.

"I'm afraid so," Mrs. Castle replied. "My husband drove down to the site. He told me that the tree is enormous and is lying at an angle across the road. Bulletins are being issued over the Charlottesville radio stations and a patrol car has been stationed along Route 250 to prevent travelers from using the road."

"And are all of your rooms rented for the night?" Caine asked. "Do you have any extra ones available?"

Mrs. Castle shook her head. "We're completely full up." She glanced at Juliet's stricken face. "Now, don't you worry about the storm, dear. You'll be perfectly safe here. And I'm sure they'll have the road cleared by noon tomorrow."

Someone called to her from another table, and Mrs. Castle bustled off, leaving Juliet and Caine alone once more. Juliet twisted her napkin and deliberately avoided Caine's eyes. They sat in silence for a long moment before Caine finally spoke.

"Mrs. Castle misinterpreted the cause of anxiety in those big blue eyes of yours, didn't she, Juliet? It's not the storm that has you worried. It's the thought of spending the night with me." He gave a light, mocking laugh. "Let me assure you that your virtue is perfectly safe, little girl. I have no intention of forcing myself on you."

His words stung her. "I'm not a little girl. And I'm not a neurotic Victorian maiden fearing the loss of my virtue, either. I just don't care to be exploited by a—a renowned wolf!"

"Renowned wolf?" Caine had the nerve to laugh. "Tell me, Juliet, which do nubile young virgins fear the most, renowned wolves or swinging playboys?"

His dark eyes were gleaming with laughter. Despite her tension, Juliet felt a smile tug at the corners of her lips in response. "You're an idiot, Saxon." She impulsively tossed a breadstick at him, which he caught deftly as it sailed across the table.

"Old Snake Saxon hasn't lost his magic hands." He pretended to spike the breadstick.

"I saw one of the catches you made with your magic hands in a game on TV a couple of years ago. The Steelers were playing the Cincinnati Bengals and you leaped through the air like a ballet dancer and caught the ball."

Juliet smiled in reminiscence. At the time she'd been impressed that such a big man could be so graceful. And now he was here, sitting across from her at the table, watching her with warm amber eyes. A spark of heat flickered deep in the core of her. His eyes were such an unusual, intriguing color. . . .

"You only saw *one* of the catches I made?" He pretended to be insulted. "Sweetheart, I made hundreds of catches that were just as impressive."

"Your modesty is truly inspiring, Saxon."

"I have some of my better plays on videotape. I'll show them to you sometime."

"Is that the football player's equivalent of inviting a woman up to see his etchings?" she asked teasingly.

"But of course." He laughed his low, sexy laugh. "Come on, Juliet." He stood up and held out his hand to her. "Let's go to bed."

Her eyes flashed. "You're deliberately trying to rattle me, Caine Saxon." She rose from her chair and clutched her purse, ignoring his outstretched hand. "Well, it's not going to work. I'm not going to stammer and blush and otherwise make a fool of myself so you can sit back and laugh your head off."

"Excellent. I'd much rather have a feisty virgin on my hands than a nervous one."

Juliet laughed. She couldn't help herself. The man was outrageous. And then she realized that she was no longer in a panic about being stranded here for the night. Caine had put her at ease by making her laugh. He had known how apprehensive she was and had soothed her fears in a humorous, unobtrusive way.

"Why don't you call home and let your sisters know where you are while I take care of the bill and get the room key," he suggested as they walked from the dining room.

Her sisters! Juliet's eyes widened. Good Lord, she'd been so absorbed in Caine Saxon, she'd forgotten all about them. That was new. She always thought of her sisters first. Anyone else came in third.

Olivia answered the telephone on the second ring. "Julie! I've been so worried about you! Where are you? Bobby Lee heard on his CB that there's a tree down, blocking 250 west of Charlottesville."

"Uh, yes, there is, Livvy. I'm—we're sort of stranded here at the Apple Country Inn until tomorrow."

"You and Caine? For the whole night?" Livvy gulped. "In—in the same room?"

"All the rooms are booked, except this one that Caine had reserved for Grant and Randi," Juliet replied in what she hoped was a matter-of-fact tone.

"In the same bed?" squeaked Livvy.

Juliet's heart lurched. "I don't know, Livvy. I haven't seen the room yet."

"It'll have a double bed, all right. Probably with a canopy," Livvy said glumly. "It will be cozy and romantic and you'll fall madly in love and then I'll have *two* sisters who are bonkers over the Saxon brothers!"

"Livvy—"

"Julie, please don't—" Livvy sighed. "I don't even

know what to warn you against. You're about to spend the night with a gorgeous hunk who has a magnificent body and the most effective lines this side of the James River. And he's a Saxon! Oh, Julie!" Her voice rose on a wail.

"Livvy, calm down," Juliet soothed. "Nothing is going to happen."

"If you believe that, you really *are* a babe in the woods, Julie!"

Juliet decided a change of subject was definitely in order. "Livvy, is Randi home? Did she say what happened between her and Grant tonight? Is she . . . terribly upset?"

"I don't know what's going on with Randi. She came marching in here full of fire and absolutely furious with Grant Saxon. Apparently, she walked out on *him* at the inn tonight. And now she's up in her room playing songs like 'I Am Woman' and 'I Will Survive' and 'You're No Good.' It's a whole new phase."

"It sounds as if she's declared war on him," Juliet said thoughtfully. "But at least she's not crying."

"No, at least she's not crying," repeated Olivia. "But now *you're* about to get all tangled up with Caine Saxon. Do you want me to put Randi's 'Hurts So Bad' record in your room so you'll have it handy?"

"Do you think you could get me a copy of 'Send in the Clowns' instead?"

"Julie, this is no laughing matter!"

"Caine's coming, Livvy. I'll see you tomorrow. And *don't* worry about me!" She hung up the phone and watched Caine walk toward her, his large, muscular body as strong and lithe and powerful as a lion's.

A rush of warmth surged through her. Livvy didn't have to worry about her tonight. Caine Saxon was really a very nice man. He wasn't a smooth operator bent on seduction. Unless . . . he didn't want her enough to make the effort? The thought jarred her.

But it certainly made sense, a wry little voice inside her head said. Why would a renowned wolf/swinging playboy want a small-town twenty-six-year-old virgin? The man had dated Miss USA, for Pete's sake! He'd enjoyed a well-publicized fling with a television actress, he'd been photographed with a full year's worth of Playmates of the Month! And had he also had not-so-well-publicized flings with all twelve of them? she wondered. Her spirits took a definite nose dive.

"Mrs. Castle says that mugs of hot cider will be served in front of the fireplace," Caine said. He stopped directly in front of her, assessing her with those leonine eyes of his. He was very close, so close that he need only lift his hand to touch her. But he didn't. "Mr. Castle plays the piano and they're going to hold a group sing-along. Do you feel like joining in?"

"Do you?" Juliet countered. She couldn't think of anything she'd rather do less. But perhaps Caine wanted to sing and sip hot cider around the fire with the group. Why else would he have mentioned it? Perhaps he considered it a more appealing alternative than being cooped up in a bedroom with an inexperienced woman—and the sister of his brother's ex-fiancée at that.

The thought that he didn't want her was abominably painful . . . because she wanted him. The insight shook her. She didn't want to spend a chaste night in bed with Caine Saxon. She wanted to sample more of the passion they'd discovered together in the rain tonight. She wanted to follow it, to see where it all would lead. . . .

"A group sing-along, eh?" he said. "Oh well, why not?" He shrugged and forced a smile. He decided that he would rather attempt single-handedly to remove the giant pin oak from the road than to gather around a piano and sing tonight. And he'd always *loathed* hot cider.

But Juliet's lovely eyes had darkened with some emotion he couldn't quite define. Anxiety? Uncertainty? Was she still unnerved by the prospect of spending the night with him? She'd just finished talking to her sisters, and no doubt that had upset her too.

He wanted to take her into his arms and reassure her that she had nothing to fear from him, that he would never hurt her or force her into anything. But the passion that flared between them whenever she was in his arms was too volatile to risk arousing. It would be a short step from soothing her to . . . other things.

He scowled, feeling ridiculously noble. Two days ago he wouldn't have dreamed of trying to protect a woman from her own responses when she was in his arms. "Send in the Clowns." Good grief, was this the way it had happened to Grant?

"This way," they heard a voice call. A waitress dressed in a pinafore was directing the guests to a large, oak-paneled room with a piano and a roaring fire in the stone fireplace. Juliet and Caine followed the crowd inside.

Mr. Castle was leading the group in an off-key rendition of "Jeepers Creepers." Mrs. Castle handed everyone a mug of steaming hot cider with the inevitable cinnamon stick in it. Caine stifled a grimace. It occurred to him that Juliet was the only woman in the world for whom he would endure this.

The singing continued for the next half hour. Mr. Castle had a wide, eclectic repertoire. He knew and was able to play almost every song that anyone requested.

Caine hoped he looked jocular enough. He was certainly trying, although every time he gazed at

Juliet's soft mouth and sparkling blue eyes he ached for her. It was a most exquisite form of torture.

Juliet found it extraordinarily difficult to keep from melting against Caine every time their shoulders accidentally touched or their eyes met. She felt as if she were burning with a fever that only Caine's kisses could assuage, but she had to grin and sing the lyrics to "The Old Gray Mare" like a good sport. It was pure torture.

"Do you know 'Send in the Clowns'?" asked a portly middle-aged man who'd been requesting show tunes continually. Mr. Castle obligingly began to play it.

Caine and Juliet looked at each other. She started to giggle—she couldn't help it. The expression on Caine's face was priceless.

"Oh, no!" He caught her arm and fairly dragged her from the room. "I can't take it."

They were both laughing as they spilled into the hallway. Juliet grinned up at Caine, her eyes shining. "At last, a reprieve!"

"A reprieve?" He stared at her. "I thought you wanted to be there, singing along with the group."

"Not me." She shook her head. "I thought *you* did."

He groaned. "Juliet, you'll never know how much I did *not* want to be there."

She tilted her head slightly to gaze up at him through demurely lowered lashes. "Caine." She tucked her hand into his and moved closer. "Let's go to bed."

Six

The blue and white bedroom was charmingly decorated with ruffled curtains, a patchwork quilt, and a double bed with a canopy. It was small and cozy and romantic, just as Livvy had said it would be. Juliet glanced up at Caine, who stood by her side, staring at the bed.

He cleared his throat. "I'll . . . er, wash up in the bathroom while you . . . uh, get undressed, Juliet."

The bathroom door closed behind him. Juliet heard him turn the key in the lock. She stood in the middle of the room, nonplussed by Caine's sudden flight. Was he nervous? Caine Saxon? She mentally scoffed at the notion.

She wasn't nervous. Not now. She unzipped her dress and hung it carefully on a hanger in the small closet. No, she wasn't nervous at all. Somehow it felt right being here with Caine. She felt safe. Her body began to tingle with anticipatory excitement. She felt safe, yet more excited and alive than she'd ever felt in her life. It should have been an odd contradiction, but it wasn't. Not at all.

Her dress was fully lined, so she'd worn no slip. She frowned a little as she removed her panty hose. Such a utilitarian, sexless garment, she thought. Olivia and Miranda had taken to wearing stockings with a garter belt, and Juliet blushed as the full impact of it all struck her for the first time. Livvy and Randi dressed—and undressed—for their lovers.

Stripped to her apricot-colored chemise and matching panties, Juliet stared at the bathroom door, which remained tightly closed. She heard water running. Caine must be taking a shower, she thought. Her gaze flicked to the bed. She felt the need to do something to assuage the tension that was slowly building inside her, so she carefully folded the quilt, put it on a chair, then turned down the covers on the bed.

Next she walked to the window to stare out at the storm. The wind seemed to have died down, but it was still raining hard. She heard a creak and whirled around. Caine was standing in the open doorway to the bathroom, a thick white towel wrapped around his waist.

Juliet stared at him, her gaze raking him from head to foot, from his damp chestnut hair to his broad, naked chest, his muscular arms, and powerful legs sprinkled with soft, fine hair. He looked incredibly virile and sexily masculine. Caine Saxon would be an ideal substitute for the athlete/model in those male underwear ads, she thought, and her breath caught in her throat.

She moistened her lips with the tip of her tongue, the small action unconsciously provocative. "Hi" was all she could think to say. Her voice was surprisingly husky.

A sharp throb of desire pulsated through Caine. He watched Juliet's small pink tongue flick over her lips once more, staring as one mesmerized. His gaze lowered to the rounded fullness of her breasts, so enticingly displayed in the silky apricot chemise. Her waist was small, her stomach flat, and her hips sweetly rounded. He couldn't tear his eyes away from her.

Juliet stood motionless, intensely aware of Caine's intimate scrutiny. Strangely enough, she was not at all embarrassed. She felt more conscious of her femininity than she'd ever felt before, and the admiration and desire in his eyes made her glow with pride.

"The . . . uh, bathroom's yours," he said hoarsely. His tongue felt thick. There was a fire burning in him. Damn, he thought. He hadn't felt this hot urgency at the mere *sight* of a woman since he was a very young teenager sneaking a forbidden peek at the centerfolds in his father's magazines.

He stared compulsively at her bare legs, studying their length, their shapeliness. The delicate ankles and slender calves, the rounded curves of her slim thighs. Shadowed beneath the thin silk of her panties was the dusky delta that sheltered her femininity. He wanted her so much that he ached.

Caine wanted her, Juliet thought. She saw the passion in his piercing, catlike eyes and exulted in it. He might have dated Miss USA and a year's worth of centerfold models, maybe he'd even taken them to bed, but none of that mattered anymore. The past was suddenly irrelevant. They were together now and he wanted *her*, Juliet Elizabeth Post. And she wanted him.

She took a step closer to him. Caine took a step back. For the first time she noticed that he was holding his clothes—jeans, sweat shirt, and navy cotton briefs—in his hand.

"I'll get dressed while you're in the bathroom," he said, taking another step away from her.

"Get dressed?" She stared at him. "You're going to sleep in your clothes?"

"It's quite practical to sleep in jeans and a sweat shirt. They don't wrinkle like your dress would."

Her eyes sparkled with laughter. "Don't you want me to see you in your underwear, Caine? That's not fair. You've seen me in mine."

"Juliet . . ."

She advanced toward him slowly, smiling, her eyes aglow. She was sexy and alluring, and Caine was jolted by another fierce spasm of arousal. When she stood directly in front of him and placed her hands on his chest, his own hands curved naturally around her waist.

"Juliet," he repeated, gazing down at her as she threaded her fingers through the tight black curls on his chest. His grip on her waist tightened, and Juliet realized that he was holding her in place. And she wanted to be closer to him.

"Don't send me into the bathroom, Caine," she said dreamily. "I want to stay here with you."

One of his hands slid slowly to the curve of her hip. "You're playing with fire, little girl," he said, his voice raspy, as she leaned into him. The impact of her softness was electrifying. "And I promised that I wouldn't let you get burned."

She snuggled against him and buried her face in the mat of wiry, soft chest hair. The fine hairs tickled her nose, and the clean male scent of him intoxicated her. "You mean you aren't going to touch me?"

The sight of her crimson-polished nails tangled in the dark hair on his chest captured her attention. She watched, fascinated, as her fingers smoothed along his chest to the hard nipple concealed beneath the downy mat. Boldly, she circled it with her thumb.

Caine stiffened and drew in a sharp breath. "Juliet!" He grabbed both of her hands, shackled her wrists with one big hand, and held her away from him.

"Didn't you like it?" she asked with beguiling innocence. "Don't you want me to touch you?" Her hands might be manacled, but her feet were free. She began to stroke his calf with her toes.

He looked down into her wide eyes. "There's a word for a sexy little tease like you," he said through clenched teeth. "And it isn't *virgin.*"

"That's all right, because after tonight I'm not going to be one." She smiled up at him, and Caine felt his willpower fading fast. Her smile captivated him, excited him, aroused him. And it was only one of the many potent weapons in her feminine arsenal.

"Aren't you?" he murmured huskily.

Their eyes met and locked for a timeless moment. Juliet felt a sharp stab of sensation deep in her abdomen. It was suddenly quite difficult to breathe.

"Juliet." He whispered her name as he lowered his head to hers.

She raised her face to him, wanting his kiss with every fiber of her being. Their lips touched. The kiss was gentle at first. Caine's lips brushed hers almost tentatively, until she sighed and opened her mouth under his. Their tongues touched and teased and stroked as the kiss deepened and their mouths fused hotly.

Her arms twined around his neck and her fingers explored the springy thickness of the hair at his nape. She slid her palms over the brawny muscles of his shoulders and back. "Caine! Oh, Caine . . ." Her head fell back over his arm when he lifted his mouth from hers. He buried his lips in the sensitive hollow of her throat. Her knees felt shaky and her legs seemed to have turned to rubber. It was becoming exceedingly difficult to stand,

and she clung to him to bolster her weak limbs. She felt the strongest urge to lie down. . . .

"I don't want you to be afraid, sweetheart." Caine's voice was low and gentle against her ear. "I'm not going to hurt you. I promise I'll take care of you."

Juliet cuddled closer. His words were superfluous. She had no fears. She knew he would never hurt her. She trusted him completely, she realized a little dizzily. She felt as if she had known him forever, as if she'd been waiting her whole life for him to finally come and claim her.

He scooped her up in his arms as easily as he would lift a doll and carried her to the bed. His lips quirked at the sight of the covers so carefully folded down. "You know you're really shattering the old myth of the cringing, reluctant virgin, Juliet."

"I've never been cringing or reluctant." She rubbed her cheek against the curve of his shoulder. "I've just been waiting for you, Saxon."

"My own personal Waterloo," he said wryly. He laid her down on the pale blue sheets.

"You're much too big to be Napoleon," she said. "But it's a nice change from your usual football metaphors."

He chuckled. "A *very* feisty virgin." He sat down on the edge of the bed.

Juliet lay still, waiting for him to lie down beside her. The dim light from the lamp on the bedside table cast shadows throughout the room, and the rain continued to pound against the window. She drank in the impressions, knowing that she would always remember them, as she would always remember this night.

Caine remained sitting on the edge of the bed, close beside her, the towel still fastened securely around him. Her gaze was drawn to his face. He was watching her intently, his expression thoughtful. With one long finger he reached down to flick the bright blue and silver earring that dangled against the curve of her neck.

"How long have you had your ears pierced, Juliet?"

She gaped at him. It was, most assuredly, the last thing in the world she'd expected him to say. Here they were, scantily dressed in a canopied bed in a cozy, darkened bedroom, and he casually asked when she'd had her ears pierced!

"I had them pierced during my last year in junior high," she managed to reply. "About twelve years ago."

"And did your sisters have their ears pierced at the same time?"

She nodded. "I was dying to have it done. Randi was deathly afraid of the needle and Livvy was pretty much indifferent to the whole thing." What a bizarre conversation this was, she thought, and her eyes mirrored her confusion.

"But once you had your ears pierced Olivia and Miranda went ahead and had it done too." It was a statement, not a question. Caine was watching her closely, his amber eyes never leaving her face.

"Yes. Randi actually fainted when they did her first ear. So they did the other one before they revived her." Juliet grinned at the memory.

"And your hair." He idly stroked the soft dark strands. "I remember going to some high-school function of Sophia's and seeing you triplets there. All three of you wore your hair long then, almost to your waist. When did you decide to cut it?"

"I decided that the style was too schoolgirlish for an eighteen-year-old," she said. "I had my hair cut for the first time the month before we left for college." She stared at him, clearly baffled by the odd questions. "Are you brushing up on the Post family history or something? It's not necessary, you know. I'm not going to quiz you."

"Can I safely assume that Olivia and Miranda

had their long hair cut in a similar fashion shortly after you did?" Caine persisted.

"Yes, within a week. Livvy decided that long hair was too much trouble when she saw how easy my short style was. Randi hated the idea, but she made an appointment anyway. She cried the whole time the hairdresser was cutting."

"I see."

Caine's enigmatic gaze perplexed Juliet further. She sat up a little, supporting herself on her elbows. "What do you mean, 'I see'?" she demanded.

His big hands cupped her shoulders. "Just verifying a hunch, sweetheart." He shifted his weight, turning toward her and pushing her back down against the pillows. "I've always been adept at picking up nuances and subtle trends in the pregame films."

"What?"

"Another one of my atrocious football metaphors, sweet. Lie down, Juliet." With one lithe movement, he was in bed beside her. He pulled up the covers before switching off the bedside lamp. "Tonight we're going to pretend we're married."

Juliet's heart began to thunder against her ribs. His phrasing was a little odd, but she decided that it was rather nice. She heard him fumbling in the dark and felt the mattress springs bounce as he moved about. What on earth was he doing? She didn't dare ask. Growing more nervous by the moment, she lay on her side of the bed, flat and still, her breathing shallow and her pulses racing as she waited for him to reach for her.

He didn't! The minutes passed. The waiting was interminable. She shifted slightly. Her eyes had gradually become accustomed to the darkness and she cast a covert glance at Caine, lying beside her. They were not touching, though Caine dwarfed the bed. He had tucked the top sheet and blanket between them, creating a definite barrier.

"Caine?"

"Go to sleep, Juliet."

She sat up abruptly. "But we—you—you said . . ."

"I said we were going to pretend we're married, Juliet. And we are. We're in bed strictly to sleep. Now, lie back down and go to sleep."

She didn't move. "You're not serious! Are you?" she added uncertainly.

"I'm quite serious, Juliet."

"But I thought—" She paused, caught her breath, and swallowed hard. "Don't you . . . want me, Caine?"

"I want you very much, Juliet." His voice was low and lilting in the darkness. "But when we make love—and we *will* make love, Juliet, I have no doubt of that—it will be because you want me as much as I want you."

"But I do!"

"You want to lose your virginity, sweetheart," he said a little roughly. "This seems to be the year for it. After all, both your sisters have. You've always been the leader, done things first, but this time your sisters beat you to it, didn't they? And now you're presented with a convenient time, place, and man, and you've decided to play catchup."

"Oh! That's not true at all, Caine Saxon!" She leaned across him to switch the lamp back on, then sat up and glared at him indignantly.

He sat up too. "Think about it, Juliet. You and your sisters have observed all the milestones together over the years. Some didn't involve a choice. You probably walked and talked around the same time, you got and lost your teeth about the same time, you graduated from school at the same time. But you've done everything that involved a choice around the same times too. Like getting your ears pierced and having your hair cut. And now you're determined to follow your sisters' lead and sleep with a man."

Juliet flushed with anger. "That's the stupidest thing I've ever heard! You couldn't be more wrong, Caine Saxon! I'm insulted that you think I'd hop into bed with any available male simply to—to equal some nonexistent record with my sisters."

"Are you saying that I'm the only man you want? The only man you would allow to make love to you, Juliet?" He studied her with piercing dark eyes.

He knew what answer he wanted to hear, of course. Somewhere during the course of the evening his feelings about Juliet had crystallized. He wanted her physically, yes, but he wanted something more from her as well. Something much more. Being her first lover wasn't enough for him. He wanted to be her only lover.

"I—I—" Juliet stammered, then lapsed into silence. She hadn't fully realized it until Caine himself had put it into words. He *was* the only man she wanted, the only man she could ever conceive making love to her. But to blatantly admit it to him? She felt the hypnotizing pull of his gaze, drawing her to him, making her feel helpless in his power. And if she were to admit how much she wanted him, that he was the only man she wanted . . .

"Not going to answer?" he asked, then shrugged. "Then I'll answer for you, Juliet. I *am* the only man for you and you do want me, but nevertheless, I intend to wait."

The arrogance of the man! she thought, incensed. If Caine Saxon believed he could dictate to her and expect docile submission, he was in for quite a surprise!

"Oh, *do* you?" Her temper ignited like a matchstick on flint. "Well, you're going to have a long wait, Caine Saxon. A lifetime wait, because if you think that I'm ever going to let an—an arrogant beast like you touch me, you're sadly deluded!"

His lips curved into a wry smile. "Let me get this straight, Juliet. If I don't perform on demand tonight, you'll never grant me another opportunity."

Put like that, it sounded so crass, so . . . unfair, she thought. But *he* was the one who was unfair. She felt confused and disappointed and more than a little embarrassed. And wildly, passionately angry. *And it was all his fault!* "You'll never have another chance with me, Caine Saxon, because after tonight I'm never going to see you again!" She flung the words at him.

"You'll see me."

The calm assertion enraged her further. "I won't. And don't think you can drag me into any more of your stupid reconciliation plots for Randi and Grant. She's moved into a new militant phase. My sister doesn't want or need your brother anymore, and I don't want or need you!"

"Are you challenging me to prove you wrong, Juliet?" Caine's voice was so calm that she failed to note the fire in his eyes.

"I don't care to talk to you anymore." Juliet flipped dramatically over on her side and pulled all the covers around her. "Turn out the light, please. I'm going to sleep now."

"You're used to calling all the shots, aren't you, Juliet?" He sounded amused. "If you're tired of talking, the talking has to stop. I'll bet your sisters would obediently turn out the light and go to sleep, just like you told them to." With one easy movement, he lifted her out of her cocoon of covers and laid her on her back, anchoring her in place with one incredibly strong leg. A leg that was encased in blue jeans. So that's what all the thrashing about had been, she realized. He had been getting dressed! "Let me go!" Her eyes were glittering with fury.

"I thought you wanted me to make love to you. In fact, you ordered me to do it."

"I did not! Anyway, I've changed my mind. You can just take your magic hands off me, Caine Saxon!"

She'd meant to annihilate him with her sarcasm, but Caine wasn't annihilated. He laughed instead. "Sorry, honey, your days of ruling the roost are over. I don't take orders very well." His lips caressed the curve of her ear and moved tenderly along her jawline, her throat. "But I'm very good at giving lessons." One large hand traveled over her rib cage to rest just below her breast. "And there are a few that you need to learn."

Juliet swallowed. She was suddenly very aware of the acute vulnerability of her position. Caine Saxon was big and strong. Perhaps it had been a mistake to antagonize him.

"Lesson number one." His hand slid over her stomach and down to her bare thighs. "You're not in command any longer. I'll never blindly follow your lead like your sisters have done in the past."

"I never expected you to!" she insisted, but her voice was weak. His hand slipped under the camisole and stroked her abdomen. His fingertips stretched higher to brush the undersides of her breasts with tantalizing, feather-light caresses.

Juliet felt an almost overwhelming urge to press herself into his hands. She arched a little and tried to stifle the moan welling up in her throat.

"Good," he said. "I'm glad we've straightened that out. Now, on to lesson number two." His hands curved over her breasts and he began to fondle the milky white softness until both sensitive mounds swelled and tautened under his touch. "You're going to belong to me," he said huskily. "Only to me."

He continued to caress her with maddening, rhythmic urgency, and Juliet drew in her breath as waves of heat stormed through her body. "Do you understand, Juliet?" He leaned over her, watching her mindless response to his sensual touch. "You're mine."

She closed her eyes, filled with a previously unknown hunger. The whole world had narrowed to this room, this bed. She twisted restlessly beneath his hands, still confined by the powerful strength of his thigh. "Caine." She whimpered his name in a wild little cry of need.

"It's all right, baby," he said soothingly, slipping the camisole from her with one deft motion. "I just want to see you, to look at you. . . ." His voice trailed off as he gazed down at her bare breasts. "You're beautiful, Juliet," he breathed. One long finger traced the outline of her taut nipple. "So pink and white, so hard and tight. And . . . all for me?"

She trembled with the force of the emotion rushing through her. "Yes, Caine," she whispered. "Yes." She reached out her arms and he crushed her to him. His mouth covered hers, demanding an impassioned response that she was only too eager to give. She wanted to give everything to him, to please him, to bind him to her with a kind of primitive, elemental pleasure that he would never find with anyone else.

When he lifted his mouth from hers she felt bereft. Then his lips closed over her nipple and sent shock waves of sensuous delight rolling over her. "So sweet," he murmured. "My lovely Juliet."

She couldn't suppress a moan.

"Yes, darling," he whispered. "Let me hear what I'm making you feel." He nibbled and sucked on the rosy peaks until her whole body was one aching throb.

"Do you want me, Juliet?" His voice was low and deep against her ear. He inserted his tongue inside the delicate pink shell, and she squirmed as a piercing dart of sexual excitement hit its target in her very core.

"Do you need me, Juliet?" he continued softly. "I want to hear you say it, love. I want to hear the words from you." His hands left her breasts to caress her stomach, her hips and thighs. They moved slowly, methodically, with mind-shattering sensual pressure. Up and down, over and over again.

"Yes, Caine," she cried. She felt as if every single inch of her body was sensitized and aching for him. When his hand slipped inside her panties she held her breath, and a hot flood of anticipation swept through her. "I want you. I need you!"

Her words seemed to reverberate in her head. Her blood was pounding so loudly in her ears that she could hear nothing but the primitive rhythm that was echoing in her brain. The intensity of the sensations sweeping through her was unlike anything she'd ever felt, ever imagined.

He slipped off her panties and she arched toward his hand. His magic hands, she thought dizzily, which were introducing her to a heady world of sensuous, magical delight. She uttered a wild cry as the tension built and built within her.

"It's all right, sweetheart." Caine's voice penetrated the sensual fog that enveloped her. "Just let go, love. Don't fight it, just go with it."

She did, and waves of the sweetest sort engulfed her, making her feel as if her whole body had turned to warm honey. Caine picked her up in his arms and held her against his chest, murmuring things to her, sexy words, love words, and she snuggled against him, filled with a delicious contentment.

Slowly, gradually, she began to surface. She cast a quick peek up at Caine and found his amber eyes upon her, watching her. He always seemed to be watching her, she thought dimly. He smiled at her, and she blushed. She nestled closer, turning her face into the curve of his shoulder.

"Juliet?" He cupped her chin with his fingers and tilted her head up, forcing her to meet his steady gaze. "There's no reason to feel shy with me, honey."

She stirred a little and was suddenly very aware that he was still wearing his jeans. And the undeniable evidence of his arousal was hard against her. "Aren't you—" She paused and blushed again. "You're still dressed."

"Which is the way I intend to stay. I don't dare spend a night in the same bed with you any other way. And before you ask me if I want you"—he caught her hand and pressed it against him—"here's your answer."

She felt the virile force of him and stared up into his eyes. "Then why—"

"You ask too many questions, lady," he interrupted in a mock-tough tone.

"Then why not shut me up?" she suggested, and he obliged by kissing her passionately. "Now put these on," he ordered, handing her her chemise and panties. "And don't ask me why!"

She was asking him to explain what he scarcely understood himself, he thought wryly. It was all tied up in his feelings for her, and those were evoking strange new emotions within him. He felt possessive and protective. She was so special to him that he was willing to sacrifice his own physical release until he knew that she was emotionally ready for him. He wanted to be more to her than a convenient relief of her virginity, he realized. He was hooked. He realized that too.

If his old teammates could see him now! Caine Saxon, that carefree bachelor who had so jovially teased all his friends who'd fallen into the commitment-and-monogamy trap, who'd once thrown a wake instead of the traditional stag party the night before a drinking buddy's wedding, that same Caine Saxon had tumbled into the same trap. And even more ironic, it didn't feel like a trap at all! The future—the present!—had never looked brighter.

Juliet struggled into her underwear, keenly aware of Caine's scrutiny. She was fighting a self-conscious confusion that threatened to undermine the delicious languor that had seeped throughout her body. Her thoughts bounced back and forth in a continuous interior dialogue.

Caine wanted her, she assured herself. He'd told her so and made sure she was aware of the unmistakable physical evidence of his desire. But for reasons which he did not care to share with her, he had decided against taking . . .

She blushed, and forced herself to complete the thought. Caine had decided against taking her, against taking his own fulfillment. How had he stopped himself? An unsettling little voice inside her head nagged. He had maintained his self-control while every trace of her own had been swept away. *She* couldn't have held back as Caine had. Even if she'd wanted to, even if she'd tried. The sudden realization jarred her.

She cast a quick glance at Caine. "What are you thinking, little Juliet?" he asked quietly, and she felt herself being pulled into his intense amber gaze.

Her body was his for the taking—he knew it, they both did—and now he was asking for her thoughts too. She closed her eyes and looked away, aware of her body's instant, electric response to the demand in his steady, catlike stare.

"Juliet?" One of his hands caressed the soft swell of her belly through the apricot silk. His fingers, long and strong and sure, seemed to burn through the light material that lay between them, and her body arched involuntarily. Every inch of her was beginning to burn, as if heat from a fire were flooding through her.

His hand moved higher to trace the sensitive peaks of her nipples with teasing, tantalizing slowness. They strained against the soft cloth, and Juliet remembered the warm wet feel of his mouth upon them. Her breathing quickened.

"Caine!" A moan caught in the back of her throat. Her eyes flew open and met his.

"The barriers are still there, Juliet," he said softly, "and I don't want anything to come between us. Talk to me. Tell me what you want, what you feel."

She felt almost mindless, torn between wanting and not wanting to let go, to give in completely, both physically and emotionally. Did she dare tell him that?

"I don't want to think," she heard herself whisper. "For the first time in my life I let my senses take over completely and I—" She halted abruptly.

"You what, darling?" Caine brushed his lips over hers, then moved to explore her throat and the delicate line of her collarbone to her shoulders, his mouth touching her in that same feather-light way. "Don't stop." He lifted his head.

Juliet was about to say the same thing to him. Don't stop. She wanted him to go on touching her, kissing her. She was swamped by a tide of sensual memories. She wanted what had happened to her before to happen again. And Caine was the one who made her want it. His control over her seemed absolute.

"I can't believe it's happening to me again," she said, almost dazedly. "I can't believe that I'm actually starting to want it to happen."

He gave a deep, husky laugh. "My passionate little virgin. I think you've surprised yourself tonight, haven't you, love?"

"Don't laugh at me!" She felt ridiculous tears

spring to her eyes and was aghast. Dammit, she thought. She was not going to cry! She refused to succumb to the awful and outdated stereotype of the weepy, overemotional virgin!

"I wasn't laughing at you, honey." He soothed her with his words and his hands. "Never that. I—" He paused and swallowed. A potent combination of tenderness and protectiveness welled up within him. He was on dangerous ground here. These feelings were so new to him. For the first time in his life he felt unsure of what to say and do around a woman.

"I wouldn't hurt you." The words seemed absurdly inadequate.

"And is that why you aren't going to make love to me?" Her beautiful blue eyes were wide with confusion. "Because you think you'll hurt me?"

"I made love to you tonight, Juliet. Lovemaking doesn't always have to end in intercourse."

She blushed at the word and was thoroughly disgusted with herself for doing so. "I think you're evading the issue," she said severely in an attempt to regain control of the conversation.

"I don't even remember what the issue is," he drawled. He gave his head a slight shake, as if to clear it. "You have me so confused—"

"That's exactly the way I feel," Juliet interrupted softly. "Confused."

"About the way you feel about me?"

"About the way I feel when you touch me," she corrected him. Somehow she found the words that had eluded her before, along with the courage to tell him what she felt. "Oh, I've read all about sex. Who hasn't these days? But nothing prepared me for the loss of control and restraint. The actual need! How do you make me want everything you do to me while you stay cool and calm and"—she smiled suddenly—"*dressed?*"

Her smile went to his head like a straight shot of

hundred and fifty proof whiskey. For a moment he simply stared at her, his senses reeling. They were even, he thought wryly. Nothing had prepared him for the incredible lightness in his head and in his heart when she smiled at him.

"I might've stayed dressed, but I was far from cool and calm, Juliet," he said thickly. "I'm more experienced than you are. I had to protect you. I . . . have to take care of you." He hadn't meant to tell her. The words had slipped out. If he had power over her, she had equal power over him, he acknowledged uncomfortably to himself.

He had to take care of her. Caine's words seemed to reverberate inside her head, warming her, thrilling her. Because he really did care about her? she wondered. It would seem so. Caine Saxon had definitely not made a practice of self-denial when it came to women and sex. But he had sacrificed his own satisfaction because he felt that he must protect her.

"Caine"—she snuggled up to him, like a kitten seeking attention and affection—"will you let me take care of you the way you took care of me?"

The silky material covering her felt cool and sensuous against his heated skin. She continued to nuzzle him, then lightly licked around his nipple with her small pink tongue. Caine felt fire flash through him and his brain seemed to explode.

Seconds later she was on her back and he was straddling her, holding her hands above her head with one of his own. "No, Juliet, you may not!" He smiled slowly, lazily. "On the other hand, I'm not averse to taking care of you again, my sexy and utterly irresistible little virgin."

Juliet lay still and limp afterward, as if she were coming back from a faint. Caine was holding her and smiling down at her with a tenderness that made her sigh. The self-consciousness and confusion were gone, as was her nervous awareness of her own stunning vulnerability to him.

It didn't seem quite so unnerving now, not with his amber eyes caressing her so warmly and his hands holding her, petting her lovingly. They seemed to have reached a new level of intimacy and understanding. Juliet knew that she felt closer to him now than she'd ever felt to anyone, barring her sisters, of course.

They lay together in the darkness, holding each other and talking quietly for a long while. Juliet wanted to know everything about Caine—his childhood, his football career, why he had elected to come back to his old hometown to open his restaurant instead of remaining in Pittsburgh where he was a popular celebrity with a guaranteed sportscasting job.

"Because I wanted something different," Caine replied thoughtfully. He kissed the top of her head. "And I sure did find it," he added dryly, and then his voice took on an authoritative note. "Now go to sleep, Juliet. It's very late."

She smiled in the darkness as his arms tightened around her. She felt relaxed and incredibly content lying there with him. "You know," she murmured drowsily, "you've really shattered the old myth about renowned wolves and swinging playboys tonight, Saxon."

He smiled wryly. "Smashed it to smithereens."

Seven

Olivia and Miranda were waiting at the front door
when Caine pulled his yellow Ferrari in front of the
Post house the next morning. Juliet watched her
sisters hurry down the walk toward the car and
suppressed the urge to groan. She cast a quick,
covert glance at Caine.

He was watching her watch her sisters. "They
can't wait to give you the third degree, eh?" he
asked.

She flushed and shrugged. She'd felt awkward
and strained in his presence since she had awakened to find herself wrapped around him like a
clinging vine. It was difficult to remember how
close and comfortable she'd felt with him the night
before. Everything seemed so different in the
sobering light of day. Her behavior during the
night suddenly struck her as aggressive and aban-
doned, and Caine's restraint no longer seemed
touchingly protective, but more like an outright
rejection!

She had rushed into the bathroom to shower

and dress, and had stiffly resisted Caine's attempts to caress her. He'd given up with depressingly little resistance, and they'd gone downstairs to eat breakfast, only to have Caine recognized by a rabid football fan who'd arrived at the inn that morning. Juliet ate her breakfast in silence while Caine good-naturedly talked football with his admirer.

The tree was cleared from the road and they drove back to Charlottesville with no further delay. Caine hadn't pressed her to talk during the drive. He'd seemed content to play a country station at full volume, singing along when he knew the lyrics. And now here they were, back at her house, with her sisters almost upon them—and she didn't even know if he planned to see her again!

"Julie! Are you all right?" Olivia asked pointedly as she pulled open the car door.

"We've been so worried," added Miranda, shooting Caine a wary glance.

"You can see for yourselves that your sister is fine," he said dryly. He resisted the urge to reach out and touch Juliet's flushed cheek. She'd been so nervous around him this morning that even a simple caress would probably make her jump out of her skin.

He congratulated himself on his restraint of last night. Her behavior this morning had underscored his belief that she wasn't yet ready for the kind of relationship he wanted with her. Though they'd been incredibly close last night, she seemed to feel the need for distance between them this morning. He'd allowed her that distance and hadn't pressed her to talk or touch.

Juliet felt her every nerve tighten. Was Caine going to let her walk away without even mentioning when they would see each other again? A close relationship with a man—with anyone other than her sisters—was new and uncharted territory for her. How did one know how much to give, how much to hold back? Last night Caine had told her he cared, but what did *that* mean?

Her eyes met and briefly held first Livvy's, then Randi's. She could almost read her sisters' thoughts. They were concerned for her, were feeling her tension, her apprehension. And then she turned to meet Caine Saxon's unfathomable amber gaze. If she only knew what *he* was thinking! It was so confusing, so frustrating. She could hold her own as part of a set of triplets, but as one lone woman in relation to one lone man, she felt hopelessly adrift.

She started to get out of the car to join her sisters, but Caine reached across the seat and grasped her wrist. Her heart jumped.

"Aren't you going to kiss me good-bye?" he asked. His voice was light.

Was he teasing her? she wondered. What kind of a response did he expect from her? She decided to play it safe and follow his lead. Light, teasing. "I thought you'd never ask," she replied in a tone that matched his, and leaned over to plant a chaste kiss on his cheek.

"When am I going to see you again?" he asked, then swore silently. He hadn't meant to rush her. He wanted to give her the time and distance she needed, but once again he had blurted out his thoughts. He was disgusted with himself. What had happened to his much-heralded finesse? This was like playing in the Super Bowl without a game plan!

"I thought you'd never ask that, either," Juliet said. She laughed and hoped that she sounded light and breezy instead of immensely relieved.

"We have to spend all day tomorrow preparing the food for the Rivingtons' party tomorrow night, Julie," Miranda inserted dampeningly.

"And I'm tied up tonight," Caine said, and frowned. "I guess that leaves this afternoon."

Juliet resisted the urge to ask exactly how and why he was "tied up tonight." If he wanted her to know, he would tell her, she lectured herself. "Do you want to play some tennis this afternoon?" she asked. "I could reserve a court at the Y."

"I've never played tennis. It's always looked a bit too energetic for me." He smiled. "After the rigors of training camp and the football season I decided a laid-back sport like golf was the one for me."

"I've never played golf."

"I'll teach you. And you can teach me tennis. I'll pick you up at one." He pulled her into his arms and kissed her soundly. "And for future reference that's the way I expect to be kissed good-bye. No more of those sisterly pecks on the cheek."

Her cheeks a warm, glowing pink, Juliet climbed from the car and turned to hurry into the house. Caine pulled away from the curb with a jaunty toot of the horn.

"Tell us everything!" Miranda demanded as she and Olivia trailed Juliet inside.

"There's nothing to tell."

"Then why is your face redder than a tomato?" Olivia teased, her eyes gleaming. "You're crazy about him, aren't you, Julie?"

"Yes," she admitted softly.

"I think you're just plain crazy," Miranda said with a frown. "Julie, he's a Saxon. Remember all those things you've been saying about the Saxon brothers?"

Juliet didn't want to talk about it. She didn't want to *think* about it. She drifted upstairs to her bedroom, leaving her sisters to stare after her, shaking their heads.

Caine arrived promptly at one, wearing lemon

yellow slacks and a blue, green, and yellow shirt. "I've never seen you quite so . . . colorful," Juliet said dryly, looking down at the white shorts, shirt, and sneakers she was wearing. "You're going to cut quite a figure on the tennis court."

"We're going golfing first. And you're supposed to be colorful for golf. For example, you should be wearing a lime green golf skirt with hot pink hippos on it and a shirt to match."

"Hot pink hippos?" She chuckled. "No thanks. I think I'll start a new trend and wear my tennis whites on the golf course."

They didn't go to the university-owned golf course that was open to the public, as Juliet had thought they would. Instead, Caine drove to Charlotteville's exclusive Farmington Country Club.

"I thought your blood had to be blue to be a member of this club," Juliet remarked as they pulled into the parking lot. There were quite a few families possessing old names and old money in Albemarle County, but the Saxons were not among them.

Caine grinned. "I merely showed them my four Super Bowl rings and I was in. I joined mainly for the golf. Sophia is the one who likes to come to all the social functions."

Juliet smiled sweetly. "I'm sure she does."

"What? No catty remarks about Sophia using the place as a hunting ground for the man of her dreams—an eighty-five-year-old millionaire with a weak heart?"

Juliet laughed. She thought Caine was right on target with that one, but she was too polite to say so. After all, Sophia was his sister.

Caine was an extremely popular member of the club, despite his lack of blue blood. Everyone spoke to him, from the caddies to the distinguished-looking older men in their outrageously colorful golf clothes to the female members of all ages. And Caine was friendly and natural with all of them, trading comments and quips with appealing ease.

No one seemed to notice her, Juliet thought, not even when Caine introduced her. It was strange to be so totally invisible. When she and her sisters were together heads turned, for the sight of identical triplets was an unusual and diverting one. And when the three of them were dressed alike jaws dropped.

Juliet felt the stirrings of unease. Caine had achieved admiration and attention on the basis of his ability as a football player and his own outgoing personality. She elicited admiration and attention simply because she'd been born one of three. On her own . . . She'd never really been on her own, she acknowledged. All through school, all through college, and now as an adult in her hometown, she was known as a Post triplet, an object of fascination.

But here at the country club no one knew she was a triplet. She was merely Caine Saxon's guest and, judging by the total indifference to which she was treated, a rather uninteresting guest at that.

"Hey, Caine, when are you going to bring Sherry Carson back?" a freckle-faced caddie of about fourteen asked him. "I still have the golf ball she autographed for me."

"Sherry dumped me," Caine replied cheerfully. "Sorry, kid, you'll just have to see her on TV."

"She was a lousy golfer, but man, oh man, what a body!" rhapsodized a slightly older caddie.

Juliet smiled bravely. Yes, Sherry Carson would have been an infinitely more interesting guest than the lone Juliet Post in her tennis whites.

"Tell the pro that I'm cutting in on his turf and giving a golf lesson today," Caine told the caddies as he chose some women's clubs for Juliet. He smiled at her. "Ready, honey?"

"As ready as I'll ever be." She was glad that Caine wasn't taking a caddie along with them. She'd heard enough about the charms of Channel 42's weather girl for one afternoon.

"Sherry Carson seems to have caused quite a stir here," she said casually as she and Caine walked out onto the links. At least she hoped she sounded casual and not jealous and insecure, which was the way she was feeling.

Caine laughed. "She sent the caddies' blood pressure rising by wearing the shortest, tightest golf skirt in the pro shop and a low-cut jersey, minus a bra. She flirted with everyone and made them promise to watch her weather forecast. I think Channel 42 had a sizable ratings' increase after Sherry's appearance here."

"I can imagine," Juliet murmured. It hurt to hear Caine talk about another woman, even jokingly. It hurt even to think of him here with another woman. But she wasn't the first woman in his life, and it was foolish to agonize over a past that she hadn't been part of. She might not be able to wow the caddies as Sherry had, but she could concentrate on learning how to play golf and on being a good companion.

And she did. All three of the Post sisters had a certain natural athletic ability—all were good swimmers and tennis players—and Juliet picked up the fundamentals of golf without much trouble.

"You've got a good, strong swing," Caine said after they'd played several holes. "With some practice you could be a really good player." He was clearly surprised by his own observation. He glanced at his watch. "It's nearly five o'clock. I never dreamed we'd stay out so long."

"Your golf lessons usually last a few minutes on the green and then a long time in the club's bar?" Juliet asked, teasing. She couldn't visualize

Sherry Carson bothering to learn to swing a nine iron or, worse, working up a sweat.

He grinned sheepishly. "Something like that. But you actually wanted to learn to play golf. You didn't once bat your eyes and ask 'Oooh, why are the balls white and not pretty colors?' or demand to sit in my lap and ride around in 'that cute little golf cart.' "

"Were you expecting me to?" she asked indignantly.

"Uh-huh. And I thought that when I'd put my arms around you to show you how to swing, you'd dissolve into mush and we'd end up necking on the fairway."

"Oh!" For a moment Juliet was too incensed to realize that he was teasing. Then she saw the glint of laughter in his eyes and advanced upon him in mock fury. "You'd better beat a strategic retreat, Saxon, before I club you with this club." She brandished her golf club like a machete.

Caine turned and ran off toward the clubhouse and Juliet chased him the whole way there, waving the club and calling out heinous threats. They drew quite a few stares from the more sedate golfers.

They were both breathless and laughing when Caine easily disarmed Juliet outside the door of the men's locker room. "I've decided to let you live," she informed him, "on the condition that you never again lump me into the vapid mush-on-the-fairway category."

His big hands closed over her shoulders and he stared down at her. The joking retort he'd been about to make died on his lips as he gazed at her flushed, upturned face. "I meant what I said about you becoming a good player," he said, his voice suddenly serious. "Will you come with me again? I'll bring my clubs along and play as I'm giving you pointers."

Somehow Juliet knew that this was something he had never said to Sherry Carson, or to any other woman. Caine Saxon was a serious athlete, and she guessed he didn't mix women with sports, not even in his leisure games.

"I'd like to," she said softly. She was exultant. "And now it's my turn to give you a lesson. A tennis lesson."

"I have to be at the restaurant by six. Our manager is off sick and I'm filling in for him." He stroked the slender curve of her neck as he spoke, and a shower of sensual sparks seemed to glow within her. "How about tomorrow?"

"I can't. We have to spend the day cooking for the Rivingtons' party tomorrow night." She sighed with real regret.

"What about tomorrow morning? Can't you escape for just an hour or two?"

His persistence thrilled her. "Maybe." She considered it. "Oh, well, why not? My sisters can spare me for a little while. From nine to ten-thirty?"

"Great! I'll pick you up at twenty of nine. We'll come here. There's a beautiful set of tennis courts on the other side of the clubhouse."

She nodded her agreement. "And wear white," she warned him. "I'll have to wash and iron my white shorts and shirt for tomorrow."

"Don't you have one of those little tennis dresses with the cute ruffled panties?" His hands settled on her waist, only to slide over her hips to cup her rounded bottom.

Juliet slipped out of his reach. There were too many people coming and going, and Caine Saxon was too well known by all of them. "Poor Caine," she teased. "How I've disappointed you! No lime green golf skirt with hot pink hippos today, and no ruffled panties tomorrow."

She tilted her head slightly to one side and grinned up at him, her blue eyes bright with laughter. Caine felt desire rise within him with shockingly swift, explosive force. She was cute and flirtatious and he wanted her. He'd actually had fun teaching her to putt, chip, and swing this afternoon. She'd been a good student, learning fast . . . and he wanted her. Everything about her appealed to him, attracted him. He wanted her, all of her, her sweet body and her laughter and her love.

He started toward her, oblivious to the people going in and out of the men's and women's locker rooms.

"Caine, look!" Juliet suddenly whispered, halting him, and he followed the direction of her gaze.

A rather large, sixty-ish matron was entering the clubhouse wearing—what else?—a lime green golf skirt printed with hot pink hippos. Caine and Juliet looked at each other and exchanged secret, conspiratorial grins. They left the clubhouse holding hands and walked the whole way to the car, talking and laughing, with their fingers tightly interlaced.

Caine arrived promptly at twenty to nine the next morning wearing white shorts, a white sweat shirt, white socks, and sneakers. "I feel like a walking commercial for Ivory Snow," he grumbled when Juliet opened the door to him. "If Coach Noll could see me now, he'd laugh his head off."

"Each sport has its own dress code," Juliet said with a smile. "For Steelers football it's black and gold and mud and blood. For golf it's bright colors, and for tennis it's white."

"While we're on the subject of sports dress codes, I have something for you." He thrust a box into her hands.

She removed the lid. Inside the box was a white tennis dress with a demure round collar, short skirt, and ruffled panties. Under the tennis outfit were a yellow shirt and a brilliant blue golf skirt printed with bright yellow whales.

"There weren't any hot pink hippos in your size," he said with mock disappointment. "But I thought that canary yellow whales were an adequate substitution."

She stared at the clothes in the box, then at Caine. "But how did you—"

"I called the pro shop at the club after I dropped you off yesterday and arranged for one of the caddies to bring the stuff down to the restaurant last night. I guessed at your size, but I'm fairly certain I got it right." His gaze swept over her. "After all, I'm quite knowledgeable about your figure," he added with a decidedly rakish grin.

She blushed, as he'd known she would. His grin broadened.

"Caine, I—I really can't accept this." She was totally flustered. "These clothes are very expensive and—"

"Would you accept them if they were cheap?"

"I—I didn't mean . . . that is . . ." She paused and took a deep breath. "It's not proper for a woman to accept personal gifts like clothing from a man," she said primly.

He laughed. He was enjoying her confusion. "No doubt your mother told you that, and her mother told *her* the same thing. Did anyone ever stop to ask why it isn't proper?"

"Well, because—because . . . "

"I have an inquiring mind, I want to know. Why is it all right for you to lie naked in my arms in bed and not all right for me to give you sports clothes?" he asked interestedly.

This time Juliet blushed all over. "Will you *please* shut up? Livvy and Randi are right in the next room!"

"If you put on the tennis dress, I swear I won't say another embarrassing word."

"That's blackmail!"

"Mmm, and so effective too."

Five minutes later Juliet rejoined him in the living room, wearing the tennis dress. "You look cute," he said, nodding his approval. "And sexy." He pulled her into his arms, and his big hand went unerringly to the ruffled panties. "I have this fantasy about you on the tennis courts—"

She quickly pulled away from him, ever conscious of her sisters, just a room away. "I have a fantasy about *you* on the tennis court," she retorted. "That I teach you to play and then beat you soundly match after match."

"Sorry, honey, it'll never happen. I'm a natural athlete and I'm a helluva lot stronger than you are. Once I pick up a few pointers you're not going to stand a chance against me."

"You didn't tell me you were an aspiring Billie Jean King," Caine said, panting, as Juliet served him another ball, which he swung at and missed. As a professional athlete he was extremely well coordinated, yet though he had picked up the basics of tennis fairly easily, it would take hours of practice before he could win a match against Juliet.

She was a good player, he thought, watching her with a surge of pride. She was quick and graceful and strong. He decided that he was going to enjoy playing tennis with her, even if she did win. And they would play golf together and—

His reverie was interrupted by the appearance of the club's tennis pro, a wiry, classically handsome blond in his early twenties with the most toothsome smile Caine had ever seen.

"You have a really strong backhand," the blond

god said to Juliet, favoring her with a flash of those dazzling teeth, "but I'd like to give you a couple of pointers, if I may. . . ."

Juliet smiled up at him. "Sure."

Didn't she realize that the idiot was coming on to her? Caine wondered as he watched the tennis pro instruct Juliet with—he thought—an excessive, unnecessary amount of touching. And she paid attention to his directions and smiled and seemed totally unaware that Mr. Teeth was flirting with her.

Caine wasn't a jealous, possessive man, but he felt jealousy burn through him. The urge to pick Juliet up and carry her away from the court and the other man was so overwhelming that he actually had to force himself not to do it.

"Want to hit a few volleys?" the pro asked Juliet, and she nodded with a smile.

He wasn't the type of man whose ego demanded the constant and undivided attention of the woman he was with, Caine told himself loftily. When Sherry Carson had dumped him for the math professor at that party he hadn't even tried to interfere. But *this* . . . This was too much. He decided that he couldn't endure another moment of watching the tennis pro lust after Juliet, who was, after all, *his* woman!

"We're leaving," Caine announced, striding to Juliet's side of the court. He caught her wrist. "Now." The ball, which the pro had just served to her, bounced off the court.

Juliet stared up at him, and her blue eyes widened in surprise. Why, Caine looked angry, she thought. Furious, in fact. But why? He'd seemed to be enjoying himself earlier. They'd been having such fun. But now . . .

"Come on, Juliet." He half dragged her off the court, enraged with himself for acting like a jealous, possessive fool.

"Caine, what's wrong?" she asked. She sounded genuinely confused, and Caine felt even worse. He knew damn well that she hadn't been flirting with the tennis pro, hadn't even been aware that the jerk was flirting with her. She loved tennis and believed that she'd merely been given a few tips by a pro.

Caine Saxon didn't relish the thought that he was acting like an idiot over a woman. It had never happened to him before. Through all the carefree days of his bachelorhood, his Steeler teammates had admiringly called him "Mr. Cool." If they could only see him now, dragging Juliet Post from the tennis court to get her away from a toothy, smarmy blond who wore three gold chains around his neck! Mr. Cool certainly had met his Waterloo!

They drove back to the Post house in silence. Caine rebuffed Juliet's tentative questions with monosyllabic grunts. If she hadn't figured out that he was behaving like a jealous buffoon, far be it from him to enlighten her. She finally lapsed into an unhappy silence and wondered what had gone wrong. Caine wanted to be rid of her, that much was certain. He didn't want to spend another second in her company.

When he dropped her off at the house they parted on mumbled good-byes. Caine sped off in his Ferrari and Juliet walked slowly inside to join her sisters in the preparations for the dinner party that night.

Eight

The Rivingtons had ordered a cocktail buffet for fifty, and the triplets planned the menu accordingly. Something less than a sit-down dinner but more than hors d'oeuvres. With Bobby Lee's help they loaded the van and arrived at the Rivingtons' spacious white brick house shortly before six. Preparations went smoothly, and by eight the buffet was laid out on the antique mahogany dining-room table. There was veal piccata, prosciutto with melon balls, jumbo shrimp, terrine of carrots and broccoli, pasta salad, spanakopita cookies, and one of the Posts' specialty desserts, *crème brûlée*.

The triplets returned to the kitchen as the guests began to serve themselves, but Bobby Lee stood with the door slightly ajar to watch the action in the dining room. "Hell's bells!" he exclaimed suddenly, and abruptly closed the door.

Juliet, Miranda, and Olivia exchanged apprehensive glances. Juliet's heart leaped into her throat to replace the lump that had been lodged there since Caine had dropped her off at the house that morning without a word.

All day long, as she had prepared the food with her sisters, she'd been pondering Caine's angry silence. And had come up with no answers except one—Caine had obviously decided that he didn't want to be with her. Perhaps she had bored him or turned him off with her athletic prowess. But he'd seemed pleased when she'd shown promise at golf. Then again, in golf one didn't pant and sweat and run all over the court as in tennis. Did Caine like his women to be decorative and glamorous all the time? If he did, she was in big trouble, for she hadn't the slightest idea of how to hold a man's interest while remaining relentlessly glamorous.

"It's Grant, isn't it?" Miranda's shaky voice intruded upon Juliet's gloomy speculation. "He's here with another woman, isn't he?" She pushed open the kitchen door, and all three sisters crowded around to peek through the crack.

They saw Grant Saxon, sportily dressed in plaid slacks and a bright green blazer, standing with his arm around a lovely young blonde who gazed up at him with admiring eyes. A small crowd was gathered around Grant, and he was expounding on the Post Sisters' Catering Service!

"Personally, I think the Posts overcharge," they heard him say. "And frankly, their selections aren't as exciting to taste as they are to view, if you get my drift. Take this veal . . . please." Grant paused as the group laughed politely at his small joke. "I mean, it's tender, but bland. . . ."

Bobby Lee closed the kitchen door firmly. "I think we've heard enough."

"Why would he malign us professionally?" Olivia asked in astonishment.

"How *dare* he malign us professionally?" Juliet raged.

"Oh, how could he?" Miranda wailed. "What are we going to do?"

"You're going to serve the food and smile at the guests and act like you didn't hear a word he said," Bobby Lee said calmly. "Your stuff is good, you know that. People will judge for themselves."

The triplets followed Bobby Lee's advice, but the pleasure had gone out of their work and their smiles were determinedly forced. Back in the kitchen they didn't smile at all. Miranda seemed numb. Though her eyes were dark with pain, she didn't cry or mention Grant's name. All three sisters worked in grim silence, and even the usually effervescent Bobby Lee was somber.

The hours during a working party normally flew by, but tonight they seemed to drag on interminably. Juliet was serving the *crème brûlée* when she overheard one of the guests ask Grant, "Where's your brother tonight? I know Faith and Tim invited him."

Grant, whose arm seemed perpetually glued around his little blond friend, smiled and shrugged. "Our manager is off, so Caine filled in for him down at the restaurant. I hear he's got a hot date lined up after closing." Grant winked, the blonde giggled, and the guest chortled conspiratorially.

His words hit Juliet with the intensity of a physical blow. Her hands faltered, but she forced herself to keep serving. Flinging the *crème brûlée* at Grant Saxon and running screaming from the room—her preferred course of action—would be detrimental to the Post Sisters' Catering Service, which had already come under fire tonight. So Juliet smiled and served, although she was dying inside.

Hot date. The phrase burned in her brain. Caine had already tired of her and was seeking his pleasure elsewhere, with another woman. He'd found her sexual inexperience uninteresting and easy to resist. He'd found *her* uninteresting and easy to resist! No wonder he'd dropped her off at the house this morning without a backward glance. No wonder he hadn't called her all day. He'd undoubtedly raced home to arrange for his *hot date* tonight.

"I told Randi to stay in the kitchen," Livvy whispered as she joined Juliet at the serving table. "Lord, Julie, just look at that girl hanging all over Grant. I feel like poisoning their *crème brûlée.* How I wish this stupid party would end!"

"That definitely makes three of us, Liv," Juliet said fervently.

Eventually, finally, the party *did* end, and after helping to unload the van at the Posts' house, Olivia and Bobby Lee left for his apartment. A downcast Miranda took a sleeping pill and went directly to bed. Juliet changed into her nightgown, an ankle-length blue cotton one with a peasant neckline and puffed sleeves, and tried to watch an old movie on television. It didn't hold her interest. Her mind was racing, and visions of Caine with some gorgeous, sexy beauty chased through her brain, along with worrisome images of Miranda slipping deeper into depression. Tonight wasn't the first night her sister had taken a sleeping pill to "blot out everything." Suppose she continued to feel the need to do so?

It was after one o'clock when Juliet turned off the television set to sit alone in the quiet darkness. A shaft of pale moonlight from the bay window was the only illumination in the room. She was so lost in thought that she didn't hear the first chimes of the doorbell. When it rang for the third time she roused herself with a sigh. Livvy had undoubtedly forgotten her key again. She often did.

But it wasn't her sister standing in the doorway.

Juliet stared in wide-eyed astonishment at Caine Saxon.

"Hello, Juliet." His amber eyes caressed her, lingering on the feminine curves gently shadowed by the soft cotton of her gown.

For a moment the urge to return his lazy smile was so strong that she almost did. Almost. Then she remembered his hot date and her blood began to boil. "I'm not Juliet. I'm Miranda," she blurted out impulsively.

He wasn't fooled, not for a moment. "No, you're not. You're not Miranda or Olivia. You're Juliet. My little Juliet," he added softly.

"I am not!" she snapped, and moved to close the door on him.

He blocked it with his body, stepping halfway inside to do so. "You're my enraged little Juliet," he corrected himself.

The sight of him wedged in her doorway, so big and muscular and virile in his black jeans and black polo shirt, only served to increase her ire. He reminded her of a strong, sleek panther with those yellow cat's eyes of his—which were roaming her body possessively. Her abdomen tightened in a devastating explosion of sexual awareness, and she desperately sought to suppress it with the first weapon that sprang to mind—anger.

"You have the nerve to come here after your—your hot date," she said in a low, furious voice, "and expect me to welcome you with open arms? You really do think you're God's gift to women, don't you? You and your boneheaded brother!"

"What hot date? And what has my boneheaded brother done now? Honey, please stop trying to close the door. As you might have noticed, I'm standing in the doorjamb and getting pulverized in the process."

She abruptly turned and stalked into the living room. Caine followed her, talking to her back.

"After we closed the restaurant shortly after mid-night tonight I went home, took a shower, changed clothes, and drove over here."

"Your brother said that you had a hot date tonight." She whirled around to glare at him as the infuriating realization dawned. "Me? *I'm* your hot date?" She got mad all over again.

"I told Grant I had an important date after closing tonight, Juliet." Caine was clearly amused. "He came up with 'hot' all on his own . . . the bone-head," he added, grinning.

Juliet was not about to be so easily appeased. "We didn't have a date tonight, Saxon. You never asked me. You didn't call all day." She couldn't resist the accusation and was immediately sorry that she hadn't. Those plaintive remarks told him entirely too much.

He caught her arm and pulled her around to face him. She attempted to break free, but her best efforts were negligible. Caine Saxon was an extraordinarily strong man. "Did you want me to call today?" he asked quietly.

"No!"

He pulled her closer until she was standing in front of him, so close that a sheet of paper couldn't be slipped between them. His nearness was her undoing. He filled her senses and obliterated her defenses.

"Yes," she admitted huskily.

His strong arms encircled her. "I didn't call because I didn't want to give you the chance to turn me down tonight. I knew from the moment I dropped you off here this morning that I was going to be back tonight."

She attempted to remain stiff and unyielding, then gave up and leaned against the hard, warm length of him. "What made you think I would turn you down?" She closed her eyes and laid her head on his chest. A wonderful, honeyed warmth flowed through her.

"After the way I behaved this morning? Honey, I gave you every reason to turn me down." His lips brushed the top of her head. "I acted like an unspeakable jerk. Have you forgiven me?"

She drew back a little to gaze up at him. " 'An unspeakable jerk'?" she repeated wonderingly. It had never occurred to her that his behavior this morning had been out of line. She'd immediately accepted full responsibility for their silent parting. She moistened her lips with her tongue. "Why did you act like an unspeakable jerk?"

"Because I was so damn jealous of that toothy tennis pro that I'm surprised I didn't turn green."

She stared at him incredulously. "You were jealous because the tennis pro at the club took an interest in my backhand?"

"An interest in your backhand?" Caine gave a derisive snort. "The little creep was interested in a lot more than your backhand, sweetheart. I couldn't stand the way he was looking at you and touching you and *wanting* you. And you didn't even know it, did you, Juliet? You weren't even aware that the guy was trying to make a pass at you. You were perfectly natural and sweet and polite . . . and that makes me an even bigger clod, doesn't it?"

"An unspeakable clod," she agreed with mock solemnity.

Caine laughed. "That's right."

Their eyes met and clung. Juliet was engulfed by a tidal wave of anticipation and longing as she watched Caine's mouth descend slowly to hers.

His lips hovered just above hers. "I spent the day rehearsing my apology to you, Juliet. Do you want to hear it?"

"No," she whispered. "I want you to kiss me."

He smiled. "In a minute. First I want to reassure

you that I'm not a jealous maniac who will go into a fit of temper every time you speak to another man."

"That would get rather tiresome," she said softly.

"This morning I was having a little trouble coming to terms with the fact that you can evoke emotions in me that I'd laughed at in other men. Now . . ." His tongue traced along the smooth inner warmth of her lower lip.

Her breath caught in her throat. "Now?" she prompted, touching the tip of his tongue with hers.

"Now I've come to terms with it."

His kiss was deep and lazy and delicious, warming her like potent brandy over a flame. She felt her insides melt as a simmering cauldron of heat flared within the very core of her.

The tips of her breasts hardened against his chest, and he spread his legs to draw her closer into the cradle of his thighs. His big hands cupped her bottom, lifting her, fitting her to him, and she clung to him, her body soft and pliant and clamoring with sensual urgency.

"Caine!" She cried his name when he lifted his mouth from hers and strung a series of erotic little kisses along the graceful curve of her neck. She was swamped by a rush of sensuous memories—of the incredibly wonderful feeling of Caine's callus-roughened palms stroking her smooth bare skin; of his deft, intimate caresses that brought her to the heights of physical rapture; of the honey-sweet glow that had followed as she lay relaxed and sated in his arms.

She wanted it again. And more. Tonight she wanted all of him. The throbbing evidence of his arousal burned like a brand through the material of their clothes, and Juliet felt a heady, feminine delight that he wanted her as much as she wanted him. She pressed against him provocatively, rubbing her unconfined breasts against him. Even the thin cotton of her nightgown was suddenly too much of a barrier. She wanted her breasts bare, to feel Caine's hands and lips on the swollen aching softness, on the tight nipples . . .

He scooped her up in his arms and carried her to the sofa, then sat down with her on his lap. Her arms were around his neck and she gazed at him, letting her desire shine in her eyes.

"Kiss me, Caine," she whispered.

His hands caressed her with long, leisurely strokes. "Let's talk for a while, honey. Tell me about your day."

"Talk? Is that what you do on a hot date?" She teased his jawline with soft kisses, then moved on to his cheeks, his forehead, his ears. "Don't have another attack of nobility, Saxon."

"Sorry, sweetheart, you seem to bring it out in me." He pushed down the elastic neckline of her nightgown and nibbled on her smooth white shoulder. "But if you want to make out on the sofa for a while, I'll indulge you."

She grinned at him. "How generous of you! And how brave!" It was fun to tease him. Exhilarating too. She laughed and hugged him tight. She felt sexy and happy and incredibly close to him.

Caine stared down at her, at her shining blue eyes, her sweet mouth, her softly rounded body curled up in his lap. The impact of her smile, of her touch sent a convulsive shudder rippling through his muscular frame. The emotions she aroused in him defied description. They were different, more intense yet more solid than anything he'd ever experienced before.

It was much more than sexual attraction—he was so familiar with that phenomenon he could teach a course on it!—though the physical chemistry between them was extremely potent. She might tease him about his "attacks of nobility," but he knew he would do anything for her, sacrifice everything for her, do whatever he could to make her happy.

"Oh, Juliet." His hands tightened possessively on her waist. "What have you done to me?"

"The same thing you've done to me?" she murmured softly, hopefully, as she caressed his cheeks with her fingertips. "Made you feel things, think things, *want* things that you'd never even dreamed of before?"

"Those are the symptoms, all right. So you've got it too?" He stretched the elastic and eased her nightgown to her waist, exposing her creamy, pink-tipped breasts.

Her breath caught in her throat as he cupped her breasts, filling his hands with them, kneading and stroking and fondling. "I've got it bad and that's not good?" she asked shakily, slightly reworking the old song title.

"It's good," he said hoarsely as his lips closed over the taut bud of her nipple. "It's very good."

With a swift movement he laid her down on the sofa and rolled on top of her. His mouth opened over hers and she eagerly welcomed the hot thrust of his tongue into the moist warmth of her mouth. His leg urgently parted her thighs and her nightgown slid upward to her hips, baring the silky softness of her upper thighs.

"You feel so good beneath me," he murmured. "So soft and sweet and responsive." He kissed her again, and her body arched convulsively as a flash of heat tore through her. "I want you, Juliet. I want you so much. Sweetheart, we're going to be so good together. . . ."

The sudden crashing noise seemed to come from another dimension, and both Juliet and Caine were slow to react to it. But another, extended series of slamming and banging noises caused Caine to leap to his feet.

"What in the hell . . . ?" He groped in the darkness and stumbled into the coffee table. He uttered an irritated curse.

Juliet sat up like a shot and tugged at her night-gown. Her state of dishabille made her extremely grateful for the darkness—which was abruptly ended with a blinding glare of light. Caine had flicked on one of the lamps.

A low moan sounded faintly from the hallway. Juliet and Caine exchanged glances. "Stay here," he ordered. "I'll see what's going on."

He strode out of the living room with Juliet at his heels. "Juliet, I told you to—" The sight of Miranda lying in a heap at the foot of the stairs brought his scolding to an immediate end.

"Randi!" Juliet cried, rushing to kneel beside her sister. "Oh, my God, Caine, she fell down the stairs!"

Miranda sat up slowly and stared around her. "What happened?" she asked groggily.

"You fell, Randi. Did you get hurt? Are you in pain?" Juliet gingerly examined her sister's head and arms for any sign of injury. "There's a bump on the left side of your head."

Miranda groaned. "I remember now. I got up to go to the bathroom and I made a wrong turn. First I bumped into the door to Livvy's room and then I made another wrong turn and fell down the steps."

"Good Lord!" Caine stared at her. "You definitely need some kind of light in your hallway to keep this from happening again."

"A light wouldn't have helped." Miranda shook her head, then winced and touched the bump on her temple. "I didn't have my eyes open."

"She took a sleeping pill tonight," Juliet hastened to explain. "They really knock her out."

As if to confirm her sister's words, Miranda closed her eyes and leaned against Juliet.

"She shouldn't be taking sleeping pills," Caine said disapprovingly. "And if she hit her head, we shouldn't let her go to sleep until we're sure she doesn't have some kind of serious injury." He leaned down and lifted Miranda to her feet. "Help me walk her to the kitchen, Juliet. We'll make her some coffee and give her something to eat. She has to stay awake."

"I don't want any coffee. I'm not hungry. I just want to go to bed," Miranda complained as Caine settled her in a kitchen chair. "Tell him, Julie."

Juliet had already put on the coffee. "I think Caine's right, Randi. Let me fix you a nice sandwich. How about your favorite—a BLT on toast?"

She opened the refrigerator and began to remove the necessary ingredients. Caine hovered over her shoulder and peered inside. "That's one well-stocked refrigerator you've got. You have everything in here."

She glanced at him, amused. "Would you like something to eat, too, Caine?"

"I *am* hungry." He smiled hopefully. "I haven't eaten since five this afternoon."

"You don't eat on the job? I wouldn't think that a man who owns a restaurant would ever be hungry."

"I try to grab a meal at the restaurant if we're not too busy, but tonight was a madhouse. As for my own cooking, it's pathetic. Roger, our chef, deserves full credit for The Knight Out's good culinary reputation."

"What would you like? A sandwich? An omelet? Pancakes? All of the above?"

"A stack of buttermilk pancakes sounds good. You even have the buttermilk. I'm impressed, Juliet."

She flashed a saucy grin. "Mother always taught us that the way to a man's heart is—"

"through his stomach." Caine and Juliet chorused the rest of the old cliché in unison, then laughed together.

The sound of muffled weeping drew their attention to Miranda. She was leaning her elbows on the kitchen table, her face in her hands.

"Randi, what's wrong?" cried Juliet in alarm.

"You two remind me of how it was when I used to c-cook for Grant," Miranda sobbed. "Something I'll never do again!"

"Oh, Randi!" Juliet put her arm around her sister's shoulders and sighed. "Randi had a terrible night tonight," she added, looking up at Caine. "We all did. Your brother showed up at the Rivingtons' party with a sexy little blonde who couldn't keep her hands off him." Her voice hardened. "And then he proceeded to malign our cooking! And tell a roomful of potential customers that we overcharged!"

"Juliet," Caine said quietly, "I agree Grant shouldn't have knocked your business, but keep in mind that he's been badly hurt too."

"He's right," Miranda whispered. "I did hurt Grant badly, that night at the Apple Country Inn." She gazed tearfully at Juliet. "I—I said some terrible things to him. I was furious with him for not making up with me the night that Sophia allegedly apologized. Instead, he scolded me and went out with another woman! I wanted to hurt him. I wanted to make him hurt as badly as I was hurting."

Caine frowned. "You succeeded, Miranda. He's hurting, all right. Terribly."

"Mmm, that explains the little blonde and the attacks on our business tonight," Juliet said thoughtfully. "Hell hath no fury like a macho man scorned."

"Behave, Juliet," Caine warned.

"He'll never forgive me, Julie!" Miranda wailed. "I struck him where he's most vulnerable. I'm ashamed of the things I said to him. Oh, what am I going to do?"

Frowning thoughtfully, Juliet began to mix the batter for Caine's pancakes. Suddenly she whirled around to face her sister. "Randi, I have a terrific idea. Tell Grant that it was me, or Livvy, at the Apple Country Inn that night. Tell him that one of us said whatever terrible things *you* said."

"Do you think it would work?" Miranda looked doubtful. "Grant knows who I am. He hasn't mixed me up with you or Livvy since our first few dates."

Caine had known *her* from her sisters before they'd ever had a date. The thought leaped to Juliet's mind and warmed her, but she forced herself to concentrate on Miranda's dilemma. "You can convince Grant that he actually did mix us up because he hasn't seen you alone for such a long time. I think it'll work, Randi. I think he'll *want* to believe that you didn't insult him."

Miranda brightened a bit. "Maybe it will work. If Caine doesn't tell Grant," she added on a pleading note.

"Oh, don't worry about Caine," Juliet said confidently. "You won't say a word, will you, Caine?"

He gave both sisters a reproving stare. "I've made the way I feel about these convenient switches in identity quite clear, Juliet. And now you're asking me to deceive my own brother?"

"Isn't there a song entitled 'The End Justifies the Means'?" Juliet asked. "Originally recorded by the late, great Prince Machiavelli?"

"Don't think you can charm me into your little scheme by being cute, Juliet," Caine growled.

"If cute doesn't do it, I'll try sexy." She grinned mischievously. She put her arms around Caine's waist and moved sinuously against him, standing on her tiptoes to nibble on his neck. "Is it working?" she asked hopefully a few moments later. "Are you charmed?"

He was fighting a losing battle, Caine acknowledged as the corners of his mouth curved into a reluctant smile. He couldn't resist her and she had to know it. His arms closed around her and he held her tightly against him for a moment before setting her firmly away from him. "All right, I won't say anything to Grant," he said gruffly. Having Miranda witness his easy capitulation was a trifle embarrassing. But Juliet wasn't at all shy about exclaiming her thanks and kissing him in front of a witness.

After serving her sister a sandwich Juliet made him a stack of the most delicious pancakes he'd ever tasted, then sat on his lap while he ate them. Miranda went to bed shortly afterward, seemingly without any aftereffects from her fall, and Caine and Juliet spent another hour and a half in the kitchen, drinking coffee and talking.

They traded opinions, likes, and dislikes on every conceivable subject. Their conversation proved to be as exciting and exhilarating as their lovemaking. They were still going strong when a sleepy-eyed Olivia arrived shortly before four A.M. She mumbled a quick hello and went directly upstairs to bed.

"I guess it's time for me to leave," Caine said reluctantly. "I had no idea it was so late."

"Take me home with you, Caine," Juliet said impulsively, her eyes soft with love. For she was in love with him. There was no other word to describe the stunning emotions he evoked within her. It had taken her twenty-six years to fall in love, but Caine Saxon was well worth waiting for.

She was his and she wanted to belong to him completely—physically, emotionally, every way a woman could belong to a man. She no longer feared losing her identity and autonomy in a loving merger. Caine wouldn't allow that to happen. He was too strong a man to need a woman to lose herself in his shadow. She would be one with Caine, yet would always retain her own strength, her own self.

Caine read the unspoken message shining in her eyes. The temptation to pick her up and carry her away with him was almost overwhelming. But he forced himself to be rational. "It'll be dawn soon." He touched her soft, flushed cheek. "Aren't you tired?"

She flashed an impish grin. "Saxon, I've never been less tired in my entire life."

"I probably should give you more time," he muttered, more to himself than to her. "You—"

"I don't need any more time. I don't want any more time. I love you, Caine." She put her arms around him and snuggled against him. "Please, take me with you."

How could he resist when he wanted her so much? he asked himself. There was no power on earth that could make him turn her away now. He kissed her deeply, tenderly. And then whispered huskily, "Get your things, Juliet. We're going home."

Caine lived in a sprawling brick ranch-style house in one of Charlottesville's newer, exclusive neighborhoods. As Juliet gazed around the large living room it struck her for the first time that Caine Saxon was a rich man. She recognized the high quality of the furniture, rugs, and accessories. Clearly no expense had been spared in the decor of his home.

The kitchen was a modern dream, large and bright and airy, with every appliance imaginable, all looking so new and untouched that she knew they were seldom used. Caine *had* described his own cooking as "pathetic."

Her eyes widened when he showed her the specially designed Jacuzzi room with its twelve-foot black marble tub. There were smaller bathrooms adjoining three bedrooms, which were attractively but impersonally decorated. It was clear that they were guest rooms and not often occupied. Caine's own bedroom was big enough to accommodate easily a king-size bed, which was covered with a green, black, and red geometric print spread, and the other pieces of heavy Spanish-style furniture. A comfortable chair and ottoman covered in the same material as the bedspread were tucked into a corner of the room.

Juliet held onto her canvas overnight bag and stared at the bed. She was still wearing her blue nightgown under the beige raincoat she'd tossed on as they were leaving her house. It had seemed like a waste of time to get dressed when she would be getting undressed so soon. Or so she'd thought at the time. Now she wondered if she hadn't been rather brazenly eager. Perhaps *too* eager?

She cast a covert glance at Caine, wondering what he was thinking. There had been so many women in his life. Was her main appeal for him the fact that she was a virgin? Apparently not too many of those crossed his path! Should she take advantage of the novelty factor and play the nervous innocent? It wouldn't take too much acting, she decided, for to her great self-disgust she was assailed by a genuine case of primitive virginal jitters.

"Scared?" Caine asked quietly. He took her bag from her, then divested her of her raincoat. He tossed both on the chair in the corner.

"Of—of course not!" she retorted with a bravado she was far from feeling. "After all, it's not like this is the first night I've ever slept with you. That night at the inn was."

He laughed. "That's true. You're becoming an old hand at getting into bed with me, aren't you?" His hand snaked out to fasten around her wrist, and he pulled her to him. "Those big blue eyes of yours are as round as saucers. What are you thinking, little Juliet?"

She managed a tremulous smile. "Actually, I was wondering what *you* were thinking."

"I'm thinking how beautiful you are, how desirable," he said huskily, taking her into his arms. "I'm thinking how special you are to me."

His fingers traced the line of her collarbone from her throat to her shoulders, then he carefully slipped her nightgown to her waist. Sliding his palms along her silken skin, he proceeded to push the nightgown over her hips, letting it drop into a pale blue pool at her feet.

Juliet stood before him in her pale blue panties, her heart thundering against her ribs. Caine's eyes were riveted to her uptilted breasts, which were firm and rounded and milky white. The rosy tips grew taut under his scrutiny. "And I'm thinking," he continued thickly, "that I can't play the noble protector any longer. Sweetheart, I have to have you!"

His mouth closed over hers with driving possession, and she drew a convulsive, shuddering breath as his hands cupped her breasts, his thumbs stroking her nipples into aching, hard arousal.

Juliet gave in to the intense yearning pulsing within her. All traces of apprehension and anxiety were erased in a ferocious tide of passion. She lovingly offered herself to him, opening completely to his mouth and lips and hands.

Mutely acknowledging her surrender, Caine swung her up into his arms and held her high against his chest. She pressed her face into his shirt and inhaled the clean scent of him. It went straight to her head, and she clung to him, her pulses pounding at a frantic rate. He laid her down gently in the middle of the big bed, then quickly stripped off his clothes.

How beautiful he was, she thought dizzily as she gazed at his hard, bare body. How strong and powerful and wondrously male. Caine felt her eyes upon him and misinterpreted her wide-eyed stare.

"I'm not going to hurt you, love," he said softly. "We'll take it slow and long and easy. I'll make it good for you, Juliet, I promise."

But Juliet felt no fear. His masculine size and strength beckoned and appealed to the passionate woman within her, who had been dormant and unawakened for so long. She was roused now, and filled with a loving urgency that precluded anything but the need to please her man. She wanted to give and give to him, but she wanted to take too. She wanted to take the wonderful completion he offered to her.

"I need you so badly, Juliet," he said hoarsely. His hand slipped between her thighs and his fingers probed the damp silk of her panties. "And you need me, too, love. You want me. I can feel how very much you want me, my passionate little Juliet."

He removed the scrap of lace and silk with one deft movement, and his fingers found the sensitive hollow of her inner thighs and began to trace erotic little patterns there. A fire ignited within her, sending flames of arousal to every nerve.

One long finger circled an achingly taut nipple, gently skimming over the sensitive skin surrounding the hot pink bud. Again and again he circled the throbbing peak, yet refrained from touching it directly. And he did the same to the small pulsing throb that lay deep between her thighs. Circling, teasing, yet holding back until she was twisting mindlessly with wild need.

"Please," she cried as her head tossed back and forth on the pillow. She was enveloped in a whirling hot mist, feeling, needing, wanting . . .

and only Caine could relieve the erotic tension building inside her. "Please, Caine."

"Yes, love," he soothed. "I'll take care of you. I'll give you everything you need." His mouth took her nipple, and when he began to suck she could feel the sensation deep within her womb. And then his hand slipped between her legs and his touch became concentrated and intense, holding her with a nerve-shattering rhythm of sensuous pressure.

"Are you ready for me, precious? Do you want me inside you as much as I want to be there?" He kissed her hungrily, torridly. "Deep, deep inside . . ."

"Oh, yes, Caine," she said in a throaty, sexy voice that she hardly recognized as her own.

He moved away from her for a moment, and she reached blindly for him, whimpering his name. If he left her she would surely die from the surging, melting electricity that had possessed her. She wanted . . . she needed . . .

"It's all right," he said. "I'm here." He gave a hoarse, self-mocking laugh. "For a moment there I almost forgot all about protecting you. And I promised that I would never hurt you . . ."

"I don't need protecting from me, Caine," she whispered, pressing herself tightly against him. "And I know you'll never hurt me."

"My darling!" Her loving trust, her open sweetness, were as powerful a lure as her voluptuous and passionate responses. "Juliet, sweetheart, I can't wait any longer!" He kissed her again, and his tongue entered her as he drove into her with a powerful thrust that caused her to cry out.

He lay still within her, giving her time to acclimate her body to his. She clutched at his shoulders, her eyes closed, her breathing shallow and uneven as she trembled beneath him.

"Sweetheart, are you all right?" he murmured

hoarsely. He buried his mouth in the tender hollow of her neck. "Open your eyes and look at me, love."

Deep blue eyes met dark amber ones. "Caine." She whispered his name in a kind of dazed wonder. He was a part of her—their bodies were joined as one. Her hands tightened possessively on him and a burst of exultant joy surged through her. He was hers. He belonged to her in a way that no one else ever had or would. She tightened around him with pure feminine possession. She felt strong and proud and glad to be a woman, holding the man she loved deeply within her.

Caine gazed into her eyes and a slow smile spread across his face. "You're not the least bit tense or scared. I don't think I'm going to have to worry about you, after all."

"Why were you worried?" She nipped playfully at his lips with her teeth, then teased him with her tongue. She felt wonderful, her body full, the aching emptiness relieved. "Did you think I'd swoon with an attack of the vapors or something?"

He chuckled. "Nothing quite so Victorian. But you're so small and dainty and—in case you haven't noticed—I happen to be built like an bull."

"I'm just the right size for you," she told him succinctly. "A perfect fit." She arched beneath him and clutched him tighter.

He drew in his breath sharply and began to move slowly within her. "So small and soft," he breathed, his strokes long and slow and deep. "So hot and tight and sweet. You're mine, Juliet. You were made for me, just me."

"Yes!" She clung to him as the golden flames licked through her veins, burning her, consuming her in a conflagration of scalding passion. "Caine, I love you!" she cried. "I love you!"

The white-hot intensity seemed to sweep her out of herself, to plunge her into a whirlpool of aching ecstasy and beyond, to a timeless dimension. She and Caine were suddenly rocked by a swell of glowing sweet waves that quenched the fire and set them down into a sensual sea of languid warmth. . . .

Nine

"It's true," Juliet said drowsily as she lay wrapped in Caine's arms. "What you said. It was absolutely true." She was tucked into the curve of his big, hard body and she wriggled against him, feeling as high and light as a helium-filled balloon drifting up into the sky.

"What did I say that's true? That I wouldn't hurt you?" His arms tightened around her and his voice lowered and deepened with concern. "I *didn't* hurt you, did I, love?"

She stretched luxuriously against him. "Mmm, you know you didn't."

"You cried out when I first entered you," he reminded her. His mouth curved into a tender smile, and he cupped her chin with one hand and forced her to meet his gaze. "But you managed to adjust to me quite well," he drawled teasingly.

"*Quite* well." She sighed at the memory. "It was wonderful, Caine. You were wonderful."

"*You* were wonderful, Juliet," he said softly, and took her mouth in a lingering kiss. "But you still

134

haven't told me what you meant when you said 'it's true.' "

"Remember when you told me that you could make my head spin in bed?" she murmured when he lifted his lips from hers.

He smiled. "I remember."

"Well, it's true." She grinned. "You can. And you did."

"There was another part to that statement that I didn't bother to add. You take my breath away, darling. In or out of bed. I think you always will."

"You *think?*" she teased, smiling up at him with loving eyes.

Caine gazed down at her and was filled with a surge of masculine pride and possession. She was his, only his. He was the first and only man to see her and touch her like this, the first and only man to be her lover.

He was more than a little surprised to feel this primitive and profound sense of possession. He was not by nature a possessive man. But he had never been any woman's first lover before. Except Juliet's.

"I *know* you will always take my breath away," he said with sudden conviction. He stared into the violet-blue depths of her eyes, remembering the way she'd gazed up at him as he'd first entered her, as he'd begun to move inside her.

And as he continued to gaze at her hundreds more images of her danced before his mind's eye. Juliet laughing and frowning, Juliet teasing him, arguing with him, making love with him. He saw her sleeping in his arms as she'd done last night, he saw her fussing over her sisters with loving concern. He saw her living in his house, sharing his life, bearing his children. . . .

I love her. There was simply no way around it, Caine acknowledged with a wry smile. He'd been

skirting the issue by making analogies with Napoleon and Waterloo. Now he was ready to admit it.

"Juliet?" he whispered.

Her eyes were closing heavily. "Hmm?" she
mumbled sleepily.

"Going to sack out on me, huh?" he teased.

She forced her eyes open and gave him an owllike
stare. "I'm awake," she insisted.

"But just barely." He smiled to himself. His masculine ego demanded that the woman he loved be
awake and alert when he made his declaration of
love. "Go to sleep, honey," he said softly, cuddling
her close and savoring the sweet, musky scent of
her.

There was plenty of time to tell her how he felt,
he thought. Perhaps he would combine it with a
proposal. It wasn't too soon. He'd been waiting for
her all his life. He drifted off to sleep as he planned
the romantic setting in which he would tell Juliet
of his love and ask her to be his wife.

In the first groggy seconds between sleep and
wakefulness Juliet wondered hazily where she
was. Comprehension dawned the moment she
opened her eyes and found herself wrapped around
Caine. Her face was buried in the curve of his
shoulder, one arm was flung across his chest, and
her legs were entwined intimately with his powerful, hair-roughened thighs.

He was still sleeping soundly, and she studied
him lovingly. She blushed as recollections of their
passionate union swept over her. How masterfully
he had taken her! And she had given herself to him
with a possessive urgency she'd never dreamed she
was capable of. Together they had soared into a
realm of intense ecstasy, and she thrilled at the
memory of their tempestuous passion.

She loved Caine Saxon. Their union had transcended mere physical pleasure, becoming a merging of spirit and soul. She was awed by this compelling loss of autonomy, but not at all threatened. She had never before felt like the whole, complete woman that she knew she now was.

She stretched a little, feeling wonderfully sore in certain places. Her movements roused Caine and he stirred. "Good morning, love." She savored the words as she spoke them. It was wonderful to wake in her lover's arms. She leaned up and tenderly touched her lips to his.

"Hello, sweetheart," he said huskily, and rolled her over on her back as his mouth took over the kiss and deepened it intimately.

She was immediately, deliciously aroused, and moved beneath him with the erotic, sensual rhythm she had learned so well last night. She felt his throbbing masculine response and her body sang with joy. He wanted her. He was her lover and she could make him want her as much as she wanted him.

The sudden sharp ring of the telephone was a jarring intrusion into their private world. Juliet stiffened. "Ignore it, honey," Caine mumbled, brushing her lips with his.

But the ringing didn't stop, and Juliet couldn't ignore it. "What if it's Livvy or Randi?" she said. Her sisters would assume she was here with Caine when they didn't find her in her own bedroom. She sat up and picked up the dark green telephone receiver.

It hadn't occurred to Juliet that perhaps someone might be calling for Caine. An incredibly stupid mistake, considering it was his phone in his house, she berated herself when she heard the unmistakably feminine voice on the other end of the line.

"May I speak to Caine, please?" the voice asked with cool aplomb.

"It's for you." She thrust the phone at him, rolled onto her stomach, and tried not to listen to Caine's conversation. She didn't *want* to hear him talk to another woman. But though she couldn't hear what the woman was saying, there was no way she could block out Caine's end of the conversation.

"Oh, hi. Yeah. No, I can't. Sorry. No, I don't think so. No. Maybe you'd better. Yeah. Bye."

Juliet heard him replace the receiver in its cradle. "She asked to see you, didn't she?" Her voice was slightly muffled by the pillow.

"You heard me refuse, Juliet," Caine replied quietly.

She'd been hoping that he would say the female voice belonged to a salesperson hawking magazines or aluminum siding or something. To have to face that another woman was issuing an invitation to *her* lover—as they lay in bed!—was an extremely difficult adjustment, even if he had turned the woman down.

Juliet swallowed. For the first time she fully understood why Miranda had instantly believed that Grant had gone off to Richmond with another woman. Grant had been a rich, sought-after bachelor, just like Caine. Women called the Saxon brothers. Women wanted them. . . .

"I didn't ask her to call and I said no to her," Caine said as he stroked her nape with firm, kneading fingers.

"I know. Three times! I heard you." Juliet sat up and tried to smile. "It's just that it's so hard . . ." Her voice trailed off. She would *not* turn into a suspicious, jealous shrew, she told herself firmly. If she couldn't trust Caine, their relationship would never last.

"Trust me, Juliet," he said softly, as though reading her thoughts. "You're the only woman in my life." He cupped her cheek with his palm and she turned her lips into his hand, kissing his fingers lightly. "I don't want anyone but you."

For now. The unwelcome thought flitted through her head, and Juliet quickly sought to banish it. She wouldn't let her apprehensions and insecurities poison her time alone with Caine. She managed a brave little smile that went straight to Caine's heart.

There would be no whining or crying or jealous tantrum, he thought. Her determined smile confirmed it. He knew that she had deliberately put aside the hurt, the doubts, and the jealousy. He was filled with admiration for her, with love. He wanted her to believe in him, the way he believed in her.

"Spend the day with me, Juliet." It was more of a command than a request. "Tonight too. Grant can fill in at the restaurant."

"I'd like to," she said.

"Are you hungry?" He swung his legs over the edge of the bed. He wanted to make love to her again, but the untimely phone call had effectively shattered the mood. There would be time for more lovemaking later, he consoled himself. Right now it was imperative to erase the faint traces of sadness from her beautiful blue eyes.

"A little." She stared up at him, her heart skipping a beat at the sight of his nude body. It was rugged and muscular, without an ounce of fat, his broad chest covered with a mat of wiry dark hair. She looked at his long, powerful legs, his strong arms and big hands, and felt a shiver of desire ripple through her. He was so beautiful, she thought dizzily. His body was a natural work of art that put all those marble statues in museums to shame.

He caught her staring and grinned. "Like what you see?"

She blushed. "You weren't supposed to see me looking."

He stroked her flushed cheek with his fingers. "I want you to look at me, Juliet." He suddenly lifted her from the bed and set her on her feet. "And I want you to like what you see," he added irrepressibly.

Taking her by the hand, he pulled her toward the bathroom. "You may only be a little hungry, but I'm starving, woman. Let's take a quick shower and go out to lunch."

"Lunch?"

"It's past noon."

"Past noon?" She gasped. "Why, I've never slept this late in my life!"

"You never spent a night like last night, either," he drawled. "And now you're about to take your first shower with a man." He drew her against him and ran his hands over her soft body. "You're doing a lot of things you've never done before, Juliet." His mouth took hers in a long, lingering kiss. "And I'm glad you're doing them with me. Only me."

Under the driving stream of water in the shower stall they soaped each other with incredible thoroughness, not missing a single curve or crevice or an inch of skin. Laughing, Juliet wrapped her arms around Caine's neck and pressed her soap-slicked body into his. His arms came around to hold her firmly against him.

"You're as slippery as a greased pig," he said, sliding his hands over her.

"A greased pig!" she howled, drawing back to glare at him.

"Sorry, that was the first thing that came to mind."

"Your imagery leaves a lot to be desired, Saxon. I thought all you wolf-playboys had a whole repertoire of stock romantic phrases that covered all occasions."

"Oh, we do. And when I'm being a wolf-playboy I use them." He grew suddenly serious as he gazed down at her. "But I'm not playing any kind of role with you, Juliet. When we're together I'm strictly being myself." He ran his fingers through her short, wet hair. "You're special, Juliet."

She hugged him tight. "That's the nicest thing you could ever say to me." It was, too, for when had she alone ever been special to anyone? She and Miranda and Olivia were special together as a set of triplets, but without her identical siblings, Juliet considered herself something of a nonentity.

Had Grant and Bobby Lee made Randi and Livvy feel unique and special and utterly original? she wondered. The way Caine made her feel? Not even their parents had been able to accomplish that, although the sisters didn't blame them for it. Having their first child born when they were both in their mid-forties—and turn out to be triplets!—had been a stunning shock to both Professors Post. They'd raised the girls as a single unit, but with an abundance of love.

"You look so lost in thought," Caine said softly. "What are you thinking, love?"

Juliet wanted to tell him that she loved him, but the words that had come so easily in the intimacy of the bedroom were somehow difficult to say in this tender, special moment. She didn't want Caine to feel that she was pressuring him to return the words, that she was taking advantage of the gentle mood between them to wring a declaration of love for him.

"I'm thinking that you're very special, too, Caine Saxon." It was as close as she dared to come to telling him how very much he meant to her. "And that I'm glad I'm here with you."

It was a revelation to discover that he had a streak of old-fashioned romantic traditionalism ingrained in him, Caine thought wryly, as he held

Juliet's warm, wet body close. He could tell her he loved her and propose right now—the atmosphere of tender intimacy was certainly right—but he envisioned the moment complete with candlelight and soft music and champagne. When he and Juliet told their children how Daddy had proposed to Mommy he didn't want to have to say it was in the shower!

The notion of their children, their life together, exhilarated him. "I'm glad you're here with me, too, little one," he said. His amber eyes alight, he lifted her off her feet and held her above him for a moment before letting her slide slowly down the length of his body. "There's no one else I'd rather shower with."

"No one else? Not even the Pittsburgh Steelers?" Her bright blue eyes teased him. "I thought you jocks had such a great time together in the locker room, snapping each other with towels, making anatomical comparisons, and the like."

Caine directed the shower nozzle over them, and the warm water sluiced their bodies, washing the soap suds away. "I'd rather make anatomical comparisons with you, Juliet."

He pulled her into his arms and they kissed and kissed, and Caine was on the verge of chucking romantic tradition and proposing right there in the shower stall—they could make up some suitable tale for the kids—when Juliet broke away from him with a grin.

"Poor Caine. You *are* starving, aren't you?"

He stared at her, dazed.

"Your stomach's growling." She reached up and turned off the taps. "We'd better get you some food before you collapse from hunger."

He groaned. There was something dismally unromantic about a growling stomach. He certainly didn't want his one and only marriage proposal linked with it. He would have to revert to his original plan, back to the soft lights and music and the diamond ring floating in a glass of iced champagne. . . .

It was one of those October days that seemed more like summer than fall, and when Juliet spied the swimming pool in Caine's backyard, she decided that she wanted to spend the afternoon in it.

They bought cheeseburgers—two for Caine, one for Juliet—fries, and shakes at the drive-through window of a restaurant, stopped by the Post house for Juliet to pick up her swimsuit, then had lunch on the screened-in porch overlooking the pool.

The water was heated, making the transition from dry to wet an easy one. Both Caine and Juliet were strong swimmers, and they swam a few laps for the sheer fun of it before challenging each other to races. Caine won at freestyle and breaststroke, but Juliet beat him badly at backstroke.

"Show-off," he grumbled as she hung, grinning, on to the side of the pool while waiting for him to join her. "How did such a little thing like you get such a strong stroke, anyway?"

"Race you again? Backstroke," she challenged.

"Forget it. My ego is already in shreds." He reached out and pulled her to him, lifting her up so that she had no choice but to wrap her legs around his waist and her arms around his neck. "But I'll let you make it up to me."

"And how shall I do that?"

His fingers slipped beneath the straps of her modestly cut black and yellow maillot. "By taking off your suit and swimming nude?"

"Not a chance, Saxon."

"No?" He nibbled sensuously on her shoulder. "I think I have a damn good chance, Juliet." His hands closed over her bottom and began to knead with strong fingers.

The desire that spun through her was heightened by the provocative position in which he was holding her. The feel of his wet, hair-roughened skin against her added another sensual dimension. Juliet exhaled on a moan as his lips and tongue teased the sensitive curve of her neck. She wanted him.

It was awesome, this power he held over her. He could make her want him with a look, a touch, a few huskily spoken words. The awareness of her vulnerability to this man unnerved her. She didn't want to be controlled by anyone. She was her own person with a mind and will of her own. A separate person.

"Take it off, sweet," Caine breathed against her ear. "Take off your swimsuit for me. I want you, Juliet."

"Now?" She gulped. "Right here, in the water?"

He laughed deeply, sexily. "Yes, my little innocent. Right here in the water."

It would be so easy to do as he asked. The newly awakened, passionate woman within her was hungry for him—and curious too! But the need to assert her independence was stronger.

"You'll have to put me down first," she whispered. "So I can pull it off." Had Caine been looking into her eyes, he would have seen the unholy gleam that suddenly lit them. But his own eyes were riveted to the sight of her erect nipples, straining against the slick material of her swimsuit.

The moment Caine set her on her feet, Juliet used the heel of her hand to blind him with a splash of water, then took off in a fast and frantic backstroke. In the few seconds it took for him to gather his scattered wits, she was halfway across the pool. But when he did come after her, it was in an amazingly swift freestyle stroke that enabled him to reach the side of the pool in time to snatch her ankle as she was trying to climb out of the water.

"I beat you again. I won!" Juliet was laughing triumphantly as she tried to kick out of Caine's grasp. Her momentary internal civil war was over. She'd won that too.

But Caine held on fast, his fingers locked around her slender ankle like a manacle. "I'm not laughing, Juliet. I don't like what you did."

She cast one glance at his stormy eyes and her laughter abruptly ceased. "You're angry because I beat you across the pool?" she asked, deliberately obtuse.

"That has nothing to do with it . . . as you well know."

She didn't care for his tone of voice. "Caine, let go of my ankle."

"No."

She gave a forceful but useless kick. He continued to hang onto her ankle. Her own temper began to flare. "Are you angry because I didn't strip and—and have sex with you the moment you demanded?"

His smile was hard. "Maybe."

"I suppose that Sherry Carson and all your other playmates would have whipped off their suits and jumped on top of you."

"Probably. They weren't the least bit prudish. Or childish either."

Juliet felt a rush of pure fury surge through her veins. "Like I am?"

He shrugged, let go of her ankle, and hoisted himself out of the pool. "You said it, I didn't." He walked toward the house, pausing to call over his shoulder, "Enjoy your swim, Juliet. You have the pool all to yourself."

"Good!" she flung after him, and spent the next twenty minutes swimming laps at near Olympic speed. When she finally climbed out of the pool and collapsed on a nearby chaise longue her heart was hammering and her breathing was labored from the strenuous exercise. She lay there for a while, until her pulse rate subsided and she was sure that she wasn't about to have a cardiac arrest.

"I brought you a glass of wine." Caine stood above her, a glass of white wine in his hand. He was dressed in cutoff jeans and an old Steelers T-shirt.

"We childish prudes don't drink wine," she said. "Bring me chocolate milk."

He sat down on the chaise alongside her out-stretched legs. "I didn't call you a childish prude, Juliet."

"The inference was certainly there, Saxon."

"I was . . . irritated."

"To say the least."

"Okay, I was made as hell at you. I wanted you and you splashed water in my face and took off, laughing. I realize that you're inexperienced, Juliet, but take it from me, such tactics are never appreciated."

"I'll keep that in mind," she said stiffly, fighting a sudden urge to burst into tears. "Anything else?"

"One more thing. Stop dragging other women into our relationship. No more cracks about my past playmates, as you so bitchily put it. What's past is past, Juliet. There is no one now but you and me." He ran his hand lightly along the length of her leg, and his tone lightened. "I was watching you swim. That was quite a workout you put yourself through. Ever thought of swimming the English Channel?"

He handed her the glass, and this time she took it and sipped the wine. Her hand trembled. "You're not angry anymore?"

He shook his head. "Are you?"

She drank some more of the wine. It was pleasantly cool to the taste, yet left a trail of warmth within her. "No, I'm not angry."

He smiled. "It looks like we've just survived our first lovers' quarrel."

"Is that what it was?" She felt confused. "I didn't want to fight, Caine. I—wanted—" She broke off. What *had* she wanted? She'd wanted to make love, yet hadn't wanted to surrender herself to the sexual power he held over her. But she'd given him that power willingly. She loved him!

Caine saw the confusion in her eyes and his voice softened. "It was just a lovers' quarrel, Juliet. Nothing more, nothing less. Two strong personalities are bound to strike sparks occasionally." He lifted her hand to his mouth and kissed the back of it. "Are we friends again?"

She nodded. Caine turned her hand over and pressed his lips against her palm. She felt the effects of his touch deep in the very core of her.

"And lovers?" He took the glass from her and set it on the ground, then drew her into his arms.

"Oh, yes, Caine!" This time she made no attempt to fight the passion flowing through her. Deep within her there was a knot of desire twisted so tight that it hurt.

He stood up and scooped her up in his arms. She clung to him. "Where are we going?"

"To bed." He dropped a quick kiss on her forehead.

"No. I—I want to go back into the pool." She looked up at him and blushed. "In the water."

"You don't have to, honey. You have nothing to prove. You're not prudish or childish simply because you prefer to make love in the bedroom."

She cast him a mischievous glance. "How do I know what I prefer? I need to do some experimenting before I can accurately state a preference, Saxon."

"Hmm, that's true. And you want to begin your research in the pool?"

"In the pool," she affirmed. "Caine?" Her hand lovingly smoothed over his cheek. "I'm sorry about what happened earlier."

"So am I, honey, but there's one positive aspect about fighting that you're about to learn." He smiled down at her, and there was a wealth of warmth and humor in his eyes. "Making up."

Ten

The romantic idyll continued as afternoon turned into evening. They defrosted and cooked dinner— leftovers from The Knight Out's all-you-can-eat fried chicken special—played in the pool, and made love, sometimes slowly and tenderly, sometimes with a ferocious, passionate urgency, but always with loving satisfaction.

It was rather like a honeymoon, Juliet mused as she lay languid and replete in Caine's arms. Just the two of them in their own private world, learning and teaching each other about themselves in a special atmosphere of emotional and physical intimacy. They talked late into the night, before finally falling asleep in each other's arms.

The melodic but insistent chimes of the doorbell awakened them the next morning shortly after nine. Juliet was curled up against Caine and his arm was flung possessively over her. Their eyes met, and they gazed at each other and smiled.

The doorbell sounded again. Caine glanced at the bedside clock, then at Juliet's sleep-flushed cheeks, and groaned. "Let's ignore it, honey. It's probably just some neighborhood kids selling something. If we don't answer the doorbell, they'll go away."

"We hope," she murmured sleepily. He pulled her closer and she snuggled against him with a contented sigh. The chimes stopped a few moments later.

"Looks like they took the hint," Caine said as he stroked Juliet's hair. He kissed her with a tenderness that quickly escalated into passion. "Darling, I—"

He never had a chance to complete his sentence. They both jumped as a barrage of pebbles hit the bedroom window.

Caine sat up in bed like a shot. "What the hell—" He strode to the window, nude and incensed. Another shower of pebbles hit the window, and he cursed as he threw on a white toweling robe.

"Hey, Caine!" a masculine voice called from outside. "I know you're in there. And we're not going away until you open the door! We have some good news for you."

"Julie! We know you're in there too!" This time it was a feminine voice. "Open up and let us in!"

"It's Randi!" Juliet said, hopping out of bed.

"And Grant!"

Caine and Juliet stared at each other for a moment before breaking into smiles.

"They're together!" Caine yelled. He opened the curtains a crack and called out to the insistent visitors, "Okay, we hear you. Go around to the front and I'll let you in."

Juliet snatched her canvas bag from the chair and hurried into the bathroom. "I'll get dressed and be right out."

"To be continued, Juliet," he called after her as she closed the door.

She smiled to herself. Yes, she and Caine would

continue their interrupted interlude of loving after they'd heard Randi and Grant's good news. And she could guess what it was—after a torturous separation Miranda and Grant had reconciled at last!

Juliet took a two-minute shower and pulled on a pair of cream-colored velour slacks and a matching top with a scoop neck and wide dolman sleeves. She ran a comb through her short dark hair and rushed out to the living room.

Grant was sitting on the sofa with Miranda on his lap. The square-cut diamond engagement ring was back on her sister's finger, Juliet noted with relief. Caine, still in robe and bare feet, was uncorking a bottle of champagne.

"Julie!" Miranda hopped off Grant's lap to hug her sister. "Everything is all right!" She flashed the diamond and grinned. "I finally worked up the courage to call Grant, and he came over this morning and we talked and—and we're going to be married, Julie!"

"Oh, Randi, I'm so happy for you!" Tears of joy shone in Juliet's eyes.

Grant stood up and crossed the room to stand beside the sisters. "And, Julie, I want you to know that there are no hard feelings."

Juliet stared at him blankly. She caught Caine's eye and he shrugged.

"I meant about those things you said to me at the Apple Country Inn," Grant explained. "I think I understand why you said them."

"Uh, you do?" she replied carefully.

"You were challenging me." Grant grinned. "You'd already called me a wimp for not confronting Miranda, and when that didn't work you tried more drastic measures. You were determined to goad me into a confrontation with Miranda. You knew once we were alone together . . ." He slipped his arms around Miranda's waist and pulled her against him.

"Clever girl, Juliet," Caine said dryly. He poured the champagne into four goblets and handed one to each. "I'd like to propose a toast to the happy couple. When is the wedding? Soon, I hope. I think there have been enough delays."

"We do too. We're applying for a marriage license tomorrow." Grant smiled tenderly at Miranda. "We plan to be married quietly as soon as we get it."

"Four days from today." Miranda sighed. "And this time we've decided to have a very small, private wedding with just the family. Daddy and Mother are flying up from Arizona. And there will be Julie and Livvy and Bobby Lee . . ."

"And Caine and my mother," Grant added.

"And Sophia?" Juliet dared to ask.

"I told Grant to invite her," Miranda said.

"Which I think is an incredibly generous gesture, considering the trouble she's caused," Grant said darkly. "I don't think I can ever forgive Sophia for what she did."

"She won't cause any more trouble." Miranda interjected with newfound confidence. "She won't be able to, darling. I'll never again be foolish enough to give her the chance."

"Nothing will ever come between us again, my love," Grant promised. He kissed his fiancée with a passion that made Caine and Juliet smile.

"Feeling slightly de trop?" Caine asked Juliet, slipping his arm around her waist. "Why don't we leave these two alone and . . . uh, find some way to occupy ourselves?"

Grant and Miranda slowly drew apart, gazing raptly at each other.

"*Definitely* de trop," Juliet agreed, smiling up at Caine.

"Hey, what about you two?" Grant stared from Juliet to Caine. "I could hardly believe it when Miranda told me that Julie was at your place, big brother. When did this all come about?"

"We started out as enemies forced to play on the same team," Caine explained with a grin. "We shared a common goal—getting you and Miranda back together again. Before either of us knew what had hit us, we were together ourselves." He winked at Juliet.

"Our romance sort of ricocheted off yours, I guess," Juliet added, and the four of them laughed.

"Well, since Miranda and I played Cupid for you, maybe you'd like to do a little favor for us?" Grant suggested.

"Uh-oh, here it comes." Caine gave a mock growl. "When he uses that wheedling-kid-brother tone I know I'm in for it."

"Kid brother? I'm only fourteen months younger than you," Grant retorted. "And what I'm going to ask you isn't all *that* bad! I promised Mom I'd put up her storm windows today. I know you took them down last spring and it's my turn to put them up, but"—his voice took on a distinct wheedling-kid-brother tone—"Miranda and I have things we want to do today . . ."

"Yeah, I can guess what you want to do." Caine leered and Miranda blushed.

"Caine, behave," Juliet said.

"Will you put up the windows for Mom, Caine?" Grant asked, wheedling. "I promise I'll take them down in the spring *and* put them up next fall."

"I'm going to hold you to that," Caine said. "And I'll put up the windows. Consider it another engagement present."

Grant and Miranda were delighted with Caine's acquiescence. "Thanks, Caine," they chorused, all smiles.

Juliet's own smile was a bit forced. A pang of disappointment shot through her. She'd hoped to spend today with Caine. She *needed* to be with him!

She decided then and there that it didn't really matter where they were or what they were doing as long as they were together. "I'll help you put up the storm windows, Caine," she volunteered gamely.

"That's sweet of you, honey, but I can't accept." He leaned down to kiss the tip of her nose. "It's a dirty job and I tend to get frustrated and swear a lot."

"He doesn't want you to see him at his worst quite yet, Julie," Grant said, chortling. "It might scare you off. He's still trying to impress you."

"One more word out of you, little brother, and you'll be putting up the damn windows yourself," Caine warned. He turned to Juliet. "I'll pick you up at seven tonight, sweetheart. We'll have dinner at the Boar's Head Inn."

Juliet brightened at the thought of a romantic dinner with Caine at one of Charlottesville's most exclusive and expensive restaurants. But it was still hard to say good-bye to him when she left his house with Grant and Miranda a little later that morning. Their kiss was too quick, and with her sister and his brother standing by, she was too shy to tell him that she loved him.

Juliet fretted about that omission during the short drive home—until it occurred to her that Caine hadn't once said that *he* loved *her*. She relived every moment of their time together, hoping to recall the moment when he had uttered the precious words. But, of course, she couldn't because he hadn't said them. Because he didn't love her? she wondered. A cold prickle of fear skimmed through her.

Miranda and Grant dropped her off at the Post house and continued on their way. She had nothing to worry about, Juliet lectured herself bracingly. Didn't actions speak louder than words? Caine had behaved lovingly toward her, even if he hadn't spoken the words. She mustn't torment herself with groundless negative fears and anxieties.

"Miranda-Juliet-Olivia!"

She turned at the sound of the names. Their neighbor, Mark Walsh, was hurrying down his front walk, calling to her. Mark had never attempted to distinguish one triplet from the others, and rather than making a wrong guess he used all three names when he had to address a Post, or referred to them collectively as "neighbor."

"Hi, Mark." She paused on the sidewalk and waited for him to reach her. "I'm Juliet," she supplied helpfully.

He took a deep breath. "Juliet, I guess you wouldn't want to go to the Rock-a-Mania show at the Field House with me tonight, would you?"

"Rock-a-Mania? I've heard it advertised on the radio for weeks." The concert, comprised of several moderately successful bands and singing groups, was being sponsored by the university and had been heavily promoted. She stared at Mark in surprise. She hadn't thought his tastes ran to rock 'n' roll concerts.

"Er, what about Sherry Carson?" she asked. The last time she'd seen Mark, Channel 42's lovely weather girl had been in the process of cooking him lasagna.

"Sherry isn't seeing me anymore. I proved to be too dull for her."

Juliet saw the pain in his eyes and her heart ached for him. "You're not dull, Mark," she contradicted swiftly.

"Sherry thinks so. I also don't have a lot of money and I don't drive a fancy sports car. She found it a novelty to have a brief fling with a math professor, but she decided that the cons outweighed the pros."

"Oh, Mark, she didn't say those things to you!" Juliet exclaimed in dismay.

He nodded. "I asked her why she didn't want to see me anymore and she told me exactly how she felt. I have to respect her for that." He made a brave attempt at a smile. "Anyway, she'd mentioned going to this concert, so I bought two tickets. . . ." He shrugged. "I don't suppose you'd like to go with me, would you, Juliet?"

"Oh, Mark, I'm sorry!" She was, truly. She would have liked to have said yes to cheer him up. "But I have a date tonight."

He sighed. "I figured. What about Miranda?"

"Randi just got reengaged to Grant Saxon."

"Oh, well." Mark sighed and shrugged again. "I guess I'll just give the tickets to Livvy and Bobby Lee. Would you ask one of them to come over and get them if they're interested?"

"Of course." Juliet patted his arm sympathetically. Poor Mark. How crushing to learn that your dream girl was a mercenary, shallow . . . She cast around in her mind for the proper derogatory noun. She couldn't come up with one derogatory enough.

Livvy was on the phone when Juliet entered the house. Juliet waved to her, then went upstairs to her room and switched on the radio. A slow love ballad was playing, and images of Caine immediately sprang to mind. She sank down on the bed, assailed with longing. How was she going to get through the whole day when she was already missing him?

Juliet was staring dreamily into space when Livvy burst into her room, her dark blue eyes snapping. "Julie, you're not going to believe this!"

Juliet came back to earth with a thud. "What, Livvy?"

"That was Emily Joy Everret, the president of the Friends of Mr. Jefferson Lawn and Garden Club, on the phone. She called to let us know that the club has decided to do their annual luncheon differently this year. Instead of having it at some-one's home they've decided to hold the luncheon in a restaurant. Can you guess which one?"

Juliet shook her head.

"The Knight Out! The club voted on it two weeks ago and all the arrangements have been made." Livvy raised her voice and thickened her accent, à la Emily Joy Everret. " 'Those darlin' Saxon boys have agreed to give us lil' ole gals the entire back dining room.' "

Juliet stared at her sister. "The arrangements were made two weeks ago?"

Olivia nodded. "I'm depressed, Julie. The garden club luncheon was our very first catering job. I've always felt that we had a special relationship with them. And we did!" she added crossly. "Until 'those darlin' Saxon boys' moved in on them!"

"But I told Caine that the Friends of Mr. Jefferson Lawn and Garden Club were our very first customers." Juliet thought back to their discussion at the Apple Country Inn. "Funny how you always remember your first customers," he'd said with perfect understanding. "I told him that the luncheon is sort of an anniversary for our business."

Olivia scowled. "I wonder how many more of our customers those Saxons are going to book into their restaurant."

"No matter how we feel," Juliet said, "the garden club has every right to hold their luncheon wherever they want. And Caine and Grant can hardly turn down customers. But why didn't he tell me that he'd booked the luncheon when I mentioned it?" She gnawed her lower lip anxiously. "Livvy, you don't think that he was deliberately being"— she gulped—"deceitful, do you?"

"Oh, I don't know, Julie! I'm so upset. I'm going to call Bobby Lee."

Juliet spent the next half hour wondering why Caine had neglected to mention that he'd booked the Posts' first customers into his restaurant. He'd had the ideal opportunity to tell her at the Apple Country Inn. They'd actually discussed the luncheon. But he hadn't told her. Nor had he told her in the days since. *Was* he being deliberately deceitful?

It was such a small thing, yet . . . If he would deliberately deceive her in small matters, wouldn't he tend to do so in other areas as well? She spent the *next* half hour worrying about that! All the tender and loving things he'd said to her while they were making love—did he mean them? Or had he been deceiving her then too?

Caine called at half past four. "Hello, lover," he said in a deep, husky voice that sent shivers of desire coursing along Juliet's nerve endings. "Have you missed me as much as I've missed you?"

Love surged through her, and she dismissed all her doubts. "Oh, yes, Caine." In less than three hours they would be together again, she thought. "I can't wait to see you tonight," she added impulsively.

"Mmm, me either. Unfortunately, it will have to be a little later than we'd originally planned. "Caine heaved a sigh. "A whole lot later, actually. We'll have to postpone our dinner date until tomorrow night, sweetheart. Our manager is still out and I'll have to work tonight."

Her heart fell with a resounding thud. "Oh."

There was a full minute's silence, then Caine said, "You do understand, don't you, honey? Since Saturday is our biggest, busiest night both Grant and I will have to be at the restaurant."

"Of course I understand," she said flatly. "I run a business, too, you know."

"Will you wait up for me, sweetheart? I'll come over as soon as we've closed. Around one o'clock."

"Another late hot date, hmm?" she said, making a stab at humor. It was adolescent to be so upset over a broken date, she scolded herself. She was in business herself. She fully understood the responsibilities that came with the territory.

"Will you be packed and ready to come home with me, love?" he asked softly.

She couldn't resist him. "Yes, Caine. I'll be ready and waiting for you."

Miranda arrived home in time to join Juliet, Olivia, and Bobby Lee for a quiet dinner of country ham, biscuits, and salad. She wasn't pleased to learn of the Friends of Mr. Jefferson Lawn and Garden Club's defection to The Knight Out, but she didn't blame Grant for it.

"Grant knows how sentimental we are about that annual luncheon," she said. "I'm sure Caine was the one who sweet-talked the ladies into having it at the restaurant. Before he was involved with you, of course, Julie," she added quickly. "He couldn't have known how we felt about it before then."

"That's true," Juliet agreed. But when he found out he could have mentioned it, she thought. He *should* have mentioned it. However, she refrained from voicing the silent addendum.

"Bobby," Livvy said, changing the subject, "Mark Walsh wants to give us tickets for the Rock-a-Mania concert at the Field House tonight. Do you want to go?"

"Rock-a-Mania concert?" Bobby Lee grimaced. "No thanks. I'm a loyal country fan. Let's go to a movie instead, Liv."

"Okay," she agreed. "We can catch the seven-twenty show if Julie and Randi don't mind me skipping out on the dishes."

Juliet and Miranda didn't mind, and Olivia and Bobby Lee left for the movie theater.

It was Juliet's idea to try the new recipe for the

white-chocolate-mousse cake. The results were spectacularly successful, and it was Miranda's idea to go to The Knight Out to take some sample pieces of cake to the Saxon brothers.

Juliet was reluctant. "Caine is coming here after closing," she said. "He can sample the cake then."

"Don't be afraid, Julie, I know he'll be happy to see you." With a triplet's unerring instinct, Miranda honed right into the source of her sister's reluctance. "Julie, the man is in love with you!"

Juliet swallowed. "He hasn't said so, Randi."

"He will," Miranda promised her blithely. "Now come on, Julie, let's take Grant and Caine some cake. They'll be so surprised!"

Although the visit was supposedly a spontaneous impulse to drop in, both Juliet and Miranda carefully reapplied their makeup, combed their hair, and changed their clothes before leaving the house. Juliet chose a jewel blue blouse and matching skirt, and accentuated her slender waist with a pink, yellow, and white scarf-sash. Miranda wore an apple green skirt and a green, yellow, and white silk blouse.

Juliet drove the van while Miranda balanced the cake plate on her lap. They found a parking space in the wide lot adjacent to the restaurant and were heading toward the door when Miranda froze in her tracks.

"Julie! Isn't that Sophia Saxon coming toward us?" she whispered nervously.

"Oh, great!" Juliet groaned. "Just what we need tonight—a bad omen!"

Sophia Saxon seemed equally disconcerted by the sight of two of the Post triplets. Her arm was linked through her escort's, a tall and quite handsome older man with a full head of thick silver hair.

"Hello, Sophia," Juliet said, not bothering to smile.

"Hello, Sophia," echoed Miranda, standing slightly behind her sister.

"Well, well, twins!" Sophia's escort said, appearing delighted. "You two sure look alike."

Sophia managed a brilliant, false smile. "Yes, don't they? Hello, girls," she added in syrupy tones. "Come to see Grant? And you brought him something to eat? How sweet!"

"We came to see Caine too," Miranda said.

"Caine's not there," Sophia said. "He left about fifteen minutes ago with a bosomy blonde wearing the tightest, lowest-cut black dress I've ever seen!" She glanced coquettishly at her date. "I'm very glad you didn't see her, Randall. Your eyes would have popped. I know Caine's did!"

Juliet's own eyes were flashing. "I suppose the blonde was named Darla Ditmayer? Were they on their way to Richmond?"

"I don't know what her name was or where they were going. Nor do I care to." Sophia tossed her thick brunette mane. "Shall we go, Randall?" She tugged at the man's arm while treating him to a meltingly sweet smile.

Juliet and Miranda watched them walk away. "She should go to Hollywood!" Miranda said indignantly. "She could make a fortune in wicked witch and vampire roles. Pure typecasting!"

"She doesn't have a very high opinion of our intelligence if she thinks we'd fall for the same trick twice," Juliet said dryly. "What a sister-in-law she'll make, Randi!"

"But she'll never be a threat again," Miranda said consolingly. "We're on to her now. You'll notice that neither of us even considered believing her."

Inside the restaurant both dining rooms were filled and there was a line of people waiting for tables. The sisters found Grant in the kitchen, in consultation with the chef. "Miranda!" His face lit up at the sight of her. "And . . . Livvy?" His smile faded somewhat. "I hope," he mumbled under his breath.

"It's Julie," Miranda corrected him. "And we brought our latest experiment for you and Caine to sample." She held up the plate with its thick slices of white-chocolate-mousse cake.

"It looks delicious, darling." Grant smiled at her, then turned to Juliet. "Julie, honey, Caine . . . uh, isn't here. He . . . had some business outside the restaurant to attend to. Didn't he tell me that he was seeing you later tonight?"

Juliet nodded. "He said he'd be over after you closed up tonight." She paused. "He . . . isn't here now?"

"You just missed him," Grant said quickly. "But I'll tell you what. As soon as he gets back, I'll send him over to your place. I'll stay and close up alone."

"I'll stay with you, Grant," Miranda offered. "Maybe I could help out in the kitchen."

"Great, Miranda. Now why don't you run along home, Julie? Caine won't be back for a while, and it would be foolish to wait here when you could be waiting in the comfort of your own home, eh?" Grant didn't pause once to breathe, and he ended on a slight gasp.

The stress of the Saturday-night crowd was certainly getting to Grant, Juliet thought. He seemed so tense. She decided to help him lighten up with a little joke. "Grant, is it true that Caine is out with a buxom blonde in an indecently tight, low-cut black dress?"

Grant choked. "Who told you that?"

"Your sister Sophia."

"Damn!" Grant clenched his fingers into a fist and pounded it into his opposite palm. "Somewhere in this world the evil Mr. and Mrs. Borgia are being confounded by their amiable, kind, and good-natured daughter who is really my sister. The two baby girls were accidentally switched at the hospital shortly after birth, and the Saxons got stuck with little Lucrezia! Juliet, I am truly sorry that Sophia is such a troublemaker!"

"Oh, Grant, we didn't take Sophia seriously," Miranda hastened to assure him. "After all, she isn't very inventive, using the same ploy twice."

"You didn't believe Sophia?" Grant repeated.

"Of course not," Juliet said. "We know now that she . . . er, changes the facts to suit her."

Grant took a deep breath. "You didn't believe her!" He seemed to steady himself. "What a relief!" He gave both sisters a little hug. "What a great, big damn relief!"

Eleven

Of course Grant had been apprehensive about her
reaction to Sophia's tale, Juliet thought as she
drove the van home alone shortly afterward. After
all, Miranda had ended their engagement on the
basis of a Sophia story. It was logical for him to
assume that Juliet might similarly overreact and
end her own relationship with his brother.

It wasn't until she was entering the Field House
for the Rock-a-Mania concert with Mark Walsh a
half hour later that it occurred to Juliet that
Sophia Saxon was unaware of her relationship
with Caine. Grant himself had only learned of it
that day.

"I'm glad you decided to come with me tonight,
Juliet," Mark said happily as he leafed through his
program. "I was sitting around feeling sorry for
myself. Your phone call was a welcome relief."

As Juliet had meant it to be. She'd seen the lone
light on in Mark's house when she had pulled the
van into her driveway, and had decided that it was
foolish for both of them to spend Saturday night

sitting home alone, feeling lonely. Caine wouldn't be over for hours. And there was poor Mark, depressed by Sherry Carson's cruel rejection. Juliet had decided on the spot to call Mark and offer to go to the concert with him.

They took their seats shortly before intermission. The band on stage played another number before the houselights came on and the master of ceremonies, a local disc jockey, took over the mike to announce the winners of his radio station's promotional contest.

"And now we'll draw the winners of our sister station—TV channel 42's—contest. . . ."

As the jovial voice pattered on Juliet turned to make a comment to Mark. His fingers suddenly dug into her arm. "Juliet! I see Sherry in the first row, directly in front of the stage."

Juliet winced. Poor Mark. How awful for him to see his former dream girl with another man—and at the very event to which he himself had planned to take her! She shouldn't have suggested that they come tonight. At least Mark would have been spared the misery of seeing Sherry Carson with— Juliet's eyes widened and her breath caught in her throat. With *Caine Saxon!*

It *was* Caine, sitting beside the bosomy blonde, who was poured into the tightest, lowest-cut black dress that Juliet had ever seen. That Sophia had ever seen!

The pieces were all beginning to fit together now in a horrible but crystal-clear picture. Sophia Saxon hadn't been lying about Caine's sexy date tonight. She didn't even know about Juliet Post's relationship with her brother! She had merely been making small talk. Remembering Sophia's honeyed tone and flirtatious smile confirmed it for Juliet. Sophia had been playing the coquette, not the bitch. *This* time she hadn't been trying to cause trouble.

Juliet could hardly swallow, thanks to the tight band that was forming around her throat. Yes, it all made sense now. Caine's phone call canceling their dinner date, Grant's near apoplexy when he'd heard what Sophia had told Juliet and Miranda, his great relief when they hadn't believed Sophia. It made depressingly painful sense.

Caine had tired of her and moved on to another woman, the woman who had dumped dear, sweet Mark because he wasn't rich enough to suit her expensive tastes, because he drove a Chevrolet instead of a fancy sports car. Well, Caine Saxon was a millionaire and drove a yellow Ferrari. Exactly what the mercenary Sherry wanted in a man.

Juliet watched the woman lean close to Caine and whisper something in his ear, and a pain of shattering intensity tore through her. For the first time she truly understood the depths of the suffering Miranda had undergone when she'd learned of Grant's betrayal. No wonder Miranda had behaved somewhat irrationally then. Such brutal pain could cause one to become temporarily unhinged!

Juliet's mind clouded. She slipped an icy-cold hand into Mark's. "Mark, I have to get out of here!" She hardly recognized the strangled little voice as her own. Her eyes burned as they filled with hot tears that blurred and distorted her vision. But the image of Caine and his voluptuous companion remained fixed in her mind's eye with stunning clarity.

"Juliet, the man with Sherry—that's the man you were with in the rain the other night!" Mark was aghast. "Oh, this is terrible! I'm so sorry." He placed a supporting arm around her waist and helped her to her feet. "We're getting out of here, now!"

Juliet cried the whole way home. She couldn't help herself. She was convulsed by deep, gasping sobs, and tears spilled down her cheeks in salty torrents. Caine didn't love her. He had merely wanted her, and now that he'd had her, he was ready to move on to his usual, sophisticated fare.

She'd been afraid from the first that she couldn't hold him, that she lacked what it would take to keep the interest of a man like Caine Saxon. But after the past few days she'd begun to think, to hope . . .

"Oh, Juliet, I'm sorry," Mark kept saying over and over as he handed her tissues from a box on top of the dashboard. "If only we hadn't gone to the concert in the first place. . . ."

"No, I'm glad we did, Mark," she managed to say between sobs. "It's good that I found out the truth. I wanted Caine to love me so much that I'd almost convinced myself that he did. And one should never confuse fantasy with reality."

"The man is a fool. You're a wonderful girl, Juliet," Mark said loyally.

His words brought little consolation. A wonderful girl she might be, but both Caine *and* Mark preferred the glamorous Sherry Carson.

In a desperate attempt to divert her Mark switched on the car radio and they listened to the plaintive voice of Tina Turner demanding to know what love had to do with it. Nothing, Juliet's heart cried. Nothing at all.

Her soul was lacerated by the razor-sharp realization that she was not Caine's love and never would be. Juliet Post had been a challenge to him because she was a virgin. Obviously, as far as he was concerned, when she'd lost her virginity she'd lost her appeal.

Juliet felt sick. She'd been living in a fool's paradise, hoping that Caine would fall in love with her. How could she ever expect to compete with a glamorous, sophisticated woman like Sherry Carson? And how could she expect Caine to give up women like Sherry for a woman like herself, who wasn't glamorous or sophisticated or worldly, whose main attraction to the world at large was being born a clone of her sisters?

Juliet declined Mark's offer to come inside with her. She wanted to be alone. The tears wouldn't stop. She had never cried so hard or so long in her life. She sat in the darkened living room, not bothering to switch on the lights. The darkness suited her, for her whole life had turned dark and dreary.

Livvy and Bobby Lee arrived back at the house shortly before midnight, talking and laughing about the movie they'd seen. When Livvy turned on a lamp Juliet blinked, squinting at the sudden streak of light.

"Julie!" Livvy took one look at her sister and gasped in horror. "What's wrong?" She sank down onto the sofa and put her arms around Juliet. "Julie, tell me what happened!"

Juliet tearfully poured out the whole story to her sister. Livvy was outraged. "The dirty, rotten, lying, cheating cad!" she exclaimed furiously.

"Wait a minute." Bobby Lee, who had been sitting in a chair opposite the sofa and listening quietly, spoke up. "Livvy, I heard you say those exact words to Randi when she first found out that Grant had gone to Richmond with another woman. When she *thought* Grant had gone to Richmond with another woman," he added pointedly.

"This is different, Bobby," Livvy said. "This is infinitely worse! Julie actually *saw* Caine Saxon with another woman. He blatantly lied to her about working late tonight. And not only is the man a liar and a cheat, he's a thief! He broke Julie's heart and *he stole our garden club luncheon!*"

"No, he isn't," Juliet protested with a sob. "It's not Caine's fault that he doesn't want me, Livvy. It's mine."

"Oh, Julie!" Livvy began to cry too.

When the doorbell chimed at twelve-fifteen Bobby Lee stood up and started toward the door. He glanced out the window and suddenly halted. "There's a yellow Ferrari parked out front," he said.

"Oh!" Olivia gasped, appalled. "Of all the nerve! How dare he come here after—after—"

"Don't let him in, Bobby Lee!" Juliet interrupted, her pulses pounding. She couldn't face him. Not now.

The doorbell chimed again. And again. And again. No one in the Post house moved. "Juliet!" Caine's voice sounded through the door as he began to pound on it. "Juliet, are you there?"

"Tell him no," she cried frantically. "Tell him that I'm not here, Bobby."

Bobby Lee walked to the door, frowning. Juliet shrank down against the sofa as she heard him greet Caine.

"Bobby Lee," Caine said. "I was beginning to think no one was home."

Juliet's eyes filled at the sound of his voice. Caine might need another woman to give him what she couldn't, but Juliet knew that she couldn't share him with anyone else. Much as she loved him, she would have to tell him that it was over. She needed him exclusively or not at all.

"Where's Juliet?" he asked. He sounded puzzled.

"Livvy?" Bobby Lee called. "Where's Juliet?"

"Julie's not here!" Livvy shouted back firmly.

"Wait a minute." Caine's voice sounded louder, closer.

"He's inside, Livvy!" Juliet whispered, clutching her sister's hand. "Bobby Lee must have let him in. Livvy, I can't see him. I can't bear it!"

"Don't worry, I'll get rid of him." Livvy patted her hand and stood up. Juliet watched her walk out of the living room and moments later heard her voice in the hall.

"Hello, Caine." Livvy's voice was icily controlled. "What brings you here?"

"I told Juliet I'd be over after the restaurant closed. Do you know where she is?"

"Oh, she's probably out partying somewhere," Livvy said breezily. "No doubt she forgot you were coming over. She's always in such a social whirl. It's difficult to keep track of all her dates, isn't it, Bobby Lee?"

Juliet groaned inwardly. Livvy was laying it on too thick, much too thick. Caine apparently agreed. "Would you mind telling me what's going on here?" he demanded. "Where's Juliet?"

Without waiting for a reply, he strode into the living room. Juliet willed herself to disappear. Needless to say, it didn't happen.

"Juliet!" He stood over her as she leaned back into the sofa cushions. "You've been crying!"

She didn't need to be reminded how ghastly she must look, with her swollen, red-rimmed eyes and puffy nose. She cast him a quick, covert glance from under her lashes. He was still wearing the gray suit, yellow shirt, and patterned tie she'd seen him in at the Field House. It was the first time she'd seen him in a suit, and he had a breathtaking elegance she had never known he possessed.

Because he didn't bother to get dressed up for her, she thought. He didn't have to! He didn't take *her* anywhere but bed! But he dressed up for the beauteous Sherry Carson. He took the local TV celebrity to parties, to concerts. . . .

A wild flash of anger revitalized her. Juliet jumped to her feet and faced him defiantly. She might not be able to disappear, but she could do the next best thing. "I'm not Juliet," she told him succinctly. "I'm Livvy."

Caine grimaced. "And I suppose that was Juliet in the hall with Bobby Lee?"

"Yes!" Livvy had entered the living room in time to hear her sister's bald pronouncement. Bobby Lee stood beside her, looking exasperated. "I'm Juliet. Now go home! We don't want you here."

"This is absurd!" Caine reached for Juliet, but she quickly crossed the room to stand behind Bobby Lee.

"You heard what she said," Juliet said hotly, safely out of Caine's reach. "Go away, Caine Saxon. We—we never want to see you again!"

"Will you drop the 'we'? It's for royalty and editorials and the pope." Caine moved slowly, purposefully across the room. "I'm dealing with you on a one-to-one basis, Juliet. And I want an explanation from you. Right now!"

"You can't order us around!" Livvy snapped furiously. "You make us sick!" Caine stared at her steadily, and she flushed a little and amended, "You make *me* sick."

"Why do I make you sick, Olivia?" Caine asked with maddening patience. "Why has Juliet been crying? I'm sure it all has to do with the lack of welcome I've received here tonight."

"You're damn right it does!" Olivia's voice shook with anger. "You can drop the innocent act, Caine Saxon. You've been found out. Julie *saw* you at the concert tonight with your—your blond bimbo!"

"I guess it goes without saying that none of us are ever going to watch Channel 42's weathercast again," Bobby Lee put in wryly.

Caine's eyes lit with instant awareness. "You think I went to that concert at the Field House with Sherry Carson tonight?" he asked Juliet, who was beginning to back slowly out of the room. She had hold of Bobby Lee's shirt and was pulling him along, using his stocky frame as a shield.

Olivia answered for her sister. "We don't think, we know! Julie and Mark saw you at that concert with Sherry Carson!"

A flash of pure rage crossed Caine's face. "And so history repeats itself. I'm to be condemned and hanged without a hearing." He continued to advance steadily toward Juliet, who was continuing her retreat, dragging Bobby Lee along with her. "Does anything about this scenario strike you as familiar, Bobby Lee?"

"*Everything* about this scenario strikes me as familiar, Caine," Bobby Lee replied respectfully.

"Well, here's where we depart from the script." Caine's voice was thick with fury and frustration. "I'm not as patient or as long-suffering as my brother Grant, Juliet. I'm not going to keep calling you, only to be continually put off by your sisters. I'm not going to write you letters that will be returned unopened. And I'll be damned if I'll spend an entire month haplessly listening to 'Send in the Clowns'! Oh, no, Juliet. Not me!"

Juliet gulped. He kept coming toward her and Bobby Lee, looking big and powerful and terribly angry. "No one is asking you to, Caine," she said stiffly.

He swore under his breath. "Come here, Juliet." It was an order, not a request. "We're going to settle this whole matter right now."

"There's nothing to settle. It—it's over between us, Caine." She was not at all successful in keeping the pain from her voice.

"Baby, it hasn't even begun!" he said. "Excuse me, Bobby Lee. I'm taking Juliet with me."

"No!" Juliet's grip on Bobby Lee's shirt tightened. "I don't want to go with him, Bobby. Make him leave!"

"*Me?* Make *him* leave?" Bobby Lee gave an incredulous laugh. "Julie, honey, take a look at the size of the man, then take a look at the size of me!" He jerked out of her grasp with one swift movement. "Sorry, sugar, I don't have a death wish. I want to live to get married and have children and see Willie Nelson in concert." He caught Olivia's hand. "Now, come on, Livvy. We're leaving these two to mind their own business." He dragged his protesting fiancée from the room and into the kitchen.

Caine and Juliet were left alone, facing each other. Juliet's eyes flicked to the staircase. She was only a few feet from it. If she could dash up the steps and lock herself in her room . . .

Caine's gaze followed hers. "Don't even think it, Juliet," he said coldly. "You wouldn't stand a chance." He extended his hand. "You're coming with me, Juliet. Now." His tone brooked no argument.

"No!" Anger and fear and resentment coursed through her, so confused and intermingled that she couldn't distinguish one from the other. "I'm not going anywhere with you, Caine Saxon! You broke our date to take Sherry Carson out, and then you arrive at my door, fresh from hers! What kind of a woman do you think I am?"

"I think you're an idiot!" he growled, and scooped her up into his arms. He carried her out into the crisp fall night, not bothering to fetch her a wrap.

He opened the driver's door of the Ferrari and dumped her into the bucket seat. She had no chance to escape for he climbed in after her, shifting her to the passenger seat and chaining her wrist with his fingers. With difficulty, he started the car, shifted into first, and drove away.

Twelve

"Let me go!" Juliet tried to wriggle free. "Caine, this is dangerous!" He was having a terrible time steering and shifting gears while holding on to her, but he was clearly not about to relinquish his captive. "Let me go, Saxon!" she tried again.

"When I'm ready!" he snapped back.

She tried a verbal assault. "If you think I'm such an idiot why are you kidnapping me?"

"Because, dammit, I'm an even bigger idiot. I happen to be in love with you!" Hardly the tender, romantic way he'd intended to inform her of his love, a wryly sane voice inside his head chided him. All his fine plans for an unforgettably poignant scene filled with love and romance had been cast aside, obliterated by his rage.

"Your timing is way off, Saxon," she said shakily. Tears threatened but she willed them away. "If you'd said it this morning, I might have believed you. But after seeing you with Sherry Carson tonight . . ."

"Maybe I should accuse you of cheating on me,

174

Juliet." Caine's voice was rapier sharp. "After all, you were at the concert tonight with Walsh."

"Don't try to shift the focus onto me by—"

"You went to the concert with Mark as his date," Caine interrupted, his voice rising. "While I was there strictly for business reasons." He let go of her wrist. "Did you hear me, Juliet? I was not at the concert *with* Sherry Carson. I was there because Channel 42 bought and was giving away three free dinners for two at The Knight Out, and they asked me to present the certificates to the winners. Sherry Carson was there from the station to draw the winners' names from a barrel. We happened to be seated next to each other, yes, but we were not—I repeat *not*—there together."

Juliet began to tremble as the impact of his words struck. "But—but Sophia said she saw you leave the restaurant with"—she gulped—"a sexy blonde who turned out to be Sherry Carson."

"Sophia!" Caine snorted. "And what happened the last time you and your sisters listened to Sophia, Juliet?"

Juliet's cheeks flamed. He was making her feel extremely stupid. "But this time I actually saw you with the very woman Sophia described," she whispered. "And Sherry told Mark that she wouldn't see him anymore because she wanted a man with more money and a fancy sports car."

Caine heaved a sigh. "Oh, Sherry was pouring on the charm, all right. It oozed out of her every pore. And it was probably her idea to pick me up at the restaurant to drive to the concert in the studio's limo—which we shared with five TV and radio execs."

Juliet said nothing. She felt too sick to talk.

Caine went on. "I canceled our dinner date tonight because I had to work, and that's what I was doing, Juliet. Working. The brief appearance at the concert falls under the category of public relations, as advertising for the restaurant. Do you believe me?"

Even in the relative darkness of the car she could see his amber eyes glowing with anger. "You sure as hell don't have much confidence in me, do you?" he asked. "If you think that I could leave you after everything we shared . . . Damn, why do you have such a low opinion of me, Juliet?"

She swallowed hard. She didn't have the answers to any of his questions but one. "I believe you, Caine," she forced herself to say. She had blown it, really blown it, she thought. He was furious and he had a right to be. She had displayed an appalling lack of trust. An *unforgivable* lack?

Caine swung off the road and braked the car to a stop. In front of them was a wooden sign, lit by a floodlight, on which APPLE COUNTRY INN was painted in bright red letters.

Juliet's eyes widened in surprise. She hadn't realized how far they'd driven. She'd been oblivious to everything but the tension sizzling between her and Caine. What now? she wondered, and her limbs went weak. Her blood throbbed and drummed wildly at every pulse point.

She absently rubbed at the red marks on her wrist left by his angry grip. He watched her for a moment, then lifted her wrist to his mouth and touched his lips to the soft skin. "Come inside with me, Juliet." Once again, it was not a request but a demand.

Her eyes filled with tears. "Caine, I—I—"

"Juliet." He held out his hand to enforce the order. Silently, trembling, she laid her hand in his. He led her inside the inn, where the cheerful Mrs. Castle greeted them and showed them to an upstairs room.

It was the same room where they had spent their first night together, marooned by the storm. Caine closed the door and locked it. Juliet watched him, her face pale.

He walked toward her, his eyes holding hers. "My original plan was to bring you here, where no one would know where we were, and make love to you until you were helpless and mindless and clinging. Too weak to make any protests at all. Then I was going to make all the necessary explanations. I didn't think you'd listen to me or believe me until I had you properly weakened, you see."

His face softened. "But it seems you trust me a little after all. You listened to me in the car and you told me that you believed me. I'm glad, Juliet," he added quietly.

"I wish I'd never doubted you," she burst out. "Even seeing what I saw, I should have given you a chance to explain, instead of jumping to all the wrong conclusions. You asked me to trust you, but I failed miserably at it."

He smiled slowly, his first smile since entering the Post house that night. "Let's upgrade your failing mark to a C minus with extenuating circumstances."

He stood directly in front of her and cupped her face with his hands. "I had a flash of insight a few minutes ago out in the car when I was railing about your lack of confidence in me. It's not a lack of confidence in me at all. It's a lack of confidence in yourself."

He gently tilted her head up, forcing her to meet his eyes. "Miranda displayed the same symptoms in her relationship with Grant. No doubt Olivia has, too, although she and Bobby Lee have certainly had an easier time of it."

Juliet gave a shaky little laugh. "As a trio we're unstoppable, but singly, on our own . . ."

His gaze filled with understanding. "You do such a terrific job of projecting the image of the irrepressible leader of the sought-after Post triplets that no one is aware that Juliet isn't quite sure of her own worth as a mere individual."

"It's so easy to get attention when you're an identical triplet," she explained softly. "All you have to do is to walk into a room—anywhere—as a group and all eyes are upon you. But if you walk into the same room all by yourself . . . no one looks.

"And then there's the added problem of *sustaining* interest. When the three of us are together all we have to do is stand there and smile and be identical and people are fascinated." She expelled a small sigh. "It's different without the group. You have to do a lot more than stand and smile."

"And you and your sisters worry that, separately, you don't have what it takes to sustain people's initial interest in you," Caine finished quietly.

"All those years my sisters and I were spotlighted in dancing school recitals and piano recitals and school variety shows, we knew we didn't have any talent for any of it. We knew the only reason we were chosen was because there were three of us and we looked alike and made the audience oh and ah."

She looked up at him with earnest, thoughtful eyes. "We triple-dated all through school, and when we started our catering business we thought we could succeed only if we appeared as an identical set, our usual conversation-piece selves."

She shook her head ruefully. "Holding the interest of a man like you seemed impossible for me to do all by myself. Seeing you with Sherry tonight confirmed my worst fears."

"I'm the man who's in love with you, Juliet. With only you." He brought her body slowly against his, one big hand cradling her head while he stroked her back with long, lazy caresses. "I have a lifetime interest in you, sweetheart. And I want to spend a lifetime proving it."

Juliet felt the terrible tension, the stiffness and

the misery slowly begin to drain from her. She was where she wanted to be, where she had feared she would never be again.

"You're everything I've ever wanted, Caine. The man I dreamed of, but never really expected to find. You're kind and understanding and tender . . ." Her arms tightened around him and she leaned into the strong, hard length of him.

"You're the only woman to bring out those qualities in me, Juliet. There's never been anyone like you in my life. You're totally unique." He nipped gently at her lips before skimming his tongue over them. "And heaven knows I've had enough experience with women to know when I'm really in love for the first time in my life. I *know* I've found the woman I want to spend the rest of my life with."

She drew back a little, fun and laughter shining in her vivid blue eyes. "You were doing fine until that part about all your experience with all those other women, Saxon."

A burst of pure happiness spun through her when she saw the love in his amber eyes. It was for her and her alone, she knew, and felt ashamed for ever doubting it, for doubting him. "I love you, Caine," she said huskily.

"I know you do. And I love you, Juliet. And I knew we had to straighten things out between us *tonight* or face being caught in a web of hurt and misunderstandings, like Miranda and Grant were."

"Now that we've straightened things out"—she flashed a sudden impish grin—"does that mean you're not going to ravish me until I'm helpless and mindless and clinging? What a disappointment!"

"I'd hate to disappoint a lady." His deft fingers made short work of the buttons on her blouse. He slipped the silky blue garment from her shoulders and let it float to the floor.

He trailed his hands over her arms and shoulders. "Tell me again that you love me," he demanded, brushing his knuckles over her ivory-colored camisole. Her nipples were already hard and tight and visible beneath the soft silk.

"I love you, Caine," she whispered on a sigh. Her scarf sash and skirt soundlessly hit the floor. "And I'm sorry that I—"

He ran his fingertips over her lips, silencing her. "Repeat after me. 'Caine, I'm sorry that I thought you were stupid enough to fall for a grasping broad with an obvious lust for money and sports cars.' "

Juliet laughed and dutifully repeated it. He was deliberately making light of it now, relegating the entire episode to the level of a bad joke. She would never fear the Sherry Carsons of the world again, though she and Caine might laugh at them.

Caine steered her over to the bed, and she felt the soft quilt brush her thighs. She wrapped her arms around him and nuzzled into his neck. "The last time we were here you hid out in the bathroom for ages and insisted on wearing your jeans to bed," she reminded him, wriggling sinuously under his caressing hands.

"Mmm, I remember." His hands disposed of her camisole, then slipped into her panties to remove them. "This time there will be no barriers, cloth or otherwise, between us, honey."

They wanted to touch, to taste every inch of each other. Caine felt Juliet tremble—with passion, with excitement and anticipation—wherever he touched her, and the feel of her sensitive fingers upon him drove him to heights he'd never reached before.

They spun on an upward spiral to ecstasy until they were both mad from the pleasure of it all, until the whirling urgency claimed them and sent them spinning together into the sweet planes of rapture.

They lay together, naked and intertwined and

content, for a long, long time, savoring their closeness and the bright promise of their love.

Caine was the first to break the comfortable silence. "I didn't get a chance to tell you that I ate the piece of white-chocolate-mousse cake you brought down to the restaurant. It was delicious, Juliet. Will you make it again for me sometime?"

"Sure." She playfully nipped at his shoulder. "But don't expect me to give the recipe to your chef so he can serve it at the Friends of Mr. Jefferson Lawn and Garden Club's annual luncheon. Those defectors will have to miss it."

"Uh-oh." Caine arched his brows. "Here it comes. Miranda already read me the riot act at the restaurant tonight for allegedly stealing your customers."

Juliet arched her brows too. It seemed quite an effective gesture. " 'Allegedly'?"

"I'm an innocent man, honey. I've never spoken to a single one of Mr. Jefferson's friends. Grant was the one who went out and hustled the good ladies during his breakup with Miranda. He knew the anniversary story and decided it would be a terrific act of revenge to usurp the luncheon. And it would have been," he added with a grin, "if Grant had gotten up the nerve to tell Miranda what he'd done."

"He didn't tell her?"

"Not on your life. Since she seemed to believe that I was at fault he pleaded with me to take the rap."

"Which you did."

"Hey, I wasn't about to risk having to hear 'Send in the Clowns' forty-three more times in a row. Anything to keep the peace between those two."

Juliet looked thoughtful. "It worries me a little that Grant and Randi haven't been totally honest with one another. He thinks it was I who told him off here at the Apple Country Inn, and now she thinks it was you who pirated the luncheon. Do you think they'll ever tell each other the truth?"

"I hope so. Right now they're both walking on eggshells around each other. Maybe when they've lived together and are more sure of each other, they'll come clean—and have a good laugh about it."

Juliet snuggled closer to her lover. "Caine, I want you to promise not to keep anything from me, even if it means sometimes breaking the peace between us."

"You're not afraid to fight with me, hmm?"

"No." Her eyes shone with confidence and love. "Because I know we'll always make up afterward."

"Always." Their kiss was a tender, ardent affirmation of their love. "Juliet?" Caine murmured huskily. "Will you marry me?"

"Oh, yes, Caine." She hugged him tight.

"This isn't exactly the way I'd planned to propose." He smiled as he stroked her hair. "I'd planned to wine and dine you, to romance you with dancing and candlelight and soft music, and then I'd look deeply into your eyes and make some pretty speech about true love and our destinies being intertwined."

She sighed. "It sounds lovely. Can we do it tomorrow?"

He chuckled. "I suppose we ought to have a cover story to tell our children. I can hardly admit that I proposed to their mother in bed!"

"Our children." She sighed again. The thought of having Caine's babies sent a delicious ache of longing through her. "I'd like to have at least three. Maybe four."

"I'll be happy to oblige. But, sweetheart, could we have them one at a time? I'd sort of like to ease into fatherhood gradually."

She gave him a dreamy-eyed smile. "The only

promise I can make is to keep on loving you, come what may."

"And that, sweet Juliet, is more than enough for me."

THE EDITOR'S CORNER

If there were a theme for next month's LOVESWEPT romances, it might be "Pennies from Heaven," because in all four books something wonderful seems to drop from above right into the lives of our heroes or heroines.

First, in Peggy Webb's utterly charming **DONOVAN'S ANGEL**, LOVESWEPT #143, Martie Fleming tumbles down (literally) into Paul Donovan's garden. Immediately fascinated by Martie, Paul feels she is indeed a blessing straight from heaven—an especially appropriate notion as he's a minister. But, discovering his vocation, Martie runs for cover, convinced that she is so unconventional she could never be a clergyman's wife. Most of the parishioners seem to agree: her spicy wit and way-out clothes and unusual occupation set their tongues wagging. Paul, determined as he is to have Martie, seems fated to lose . . . until a small miracle or two intervenes. You simply can't let yourself miss this funny, heartwarming love story that so perfectly captures the atmosphere of a small Southern town.

The very title of our next romance, **WILD BLUE YONDER**, LOVESWEPT #144, by Millie Grey, gives you a clue to how it fits our theme. Mike Donahue pilots an antique biplane like a barnstormer of years gone by. And when he develops engine trouble and lands on Krissa Colbrook's property, he's soon devel-

(continued)

oping trouble for her too . . . trouble of the heart. The last kind of man placid Krissa needs or wants in her life is a daredevil, yet she falls hard for this irresistible vagabond who's come to her from the sky above. We think it would be hard for a reader to fail to be charmed by Mike, so we feel secure in saying that you will be enchanted by the way Mike goes about ridding Krissa of her fears!

For just a second now try to put yourself into the very large shoes of one Morgan Abbott, hero of talented newcomer Linda Cajio's **ALL IS FAIR . . . ,** LOVESWEPT #145. Imagine that you (you're that handsome Morgan, remember?) are having dinner with acquaintances when an absolutely stunning beauty—who is also a perfect stranger—rushes up and kisses you passionately before quickly disappearing. Then, another day in another city, the same gorgeous lady again appears suddenly, kisses you senseless and vanishes. Wouldn't your head be reeling? Well, those are just two of the several unique ways that Cecilia St. Martin gets to Abbott. You will relish this wildly wonderful, very touching romance from Linda who makes her truly stylish, truly nifty debut as a romance writer with us.

And last, but never, never least is the beautiful romance **JOURNEY'S END,** LOVESWEPT #146, by Joan Elliott Pickart. In this dramatic and tender love story Victoria Blair finds everything she ever dreamed of having in the arms of Sage Lawson, owner of the Lazy L ranch just outside Sunshine, New Mexico. Indeed at times sunshine does seem to pour down on these two lovely people who appear to be made in heaven for each other. Yet ominous clouds of doubt and misunderstanding threaten their budding love. Sage

(continued)

grows hostile, Blair becomes distant, withdrawn. Clearly they need a little push back into one another's arms . . . and the matchmakers and the ways they give that little push are sure to delight you.

As always, we hope that each of these four LOVE-SWEPTs will give you the greatest of pleasure.

With warm good wishes,

Carolyn Nichols

Carolyn Nichols
   Editor
LOVESWEPT
Bantam Books, Inc.
666 Fifth Avenue
New York, NY 10103

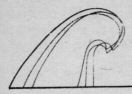 # LOVESWEPT

Love Stories you'll never forget by authors you'll always remember

 **LOVESWEPT**

Love Stories you'll never forget by authors you'll always remember

☐	21708	**Out of This World** #103	Nancy Holder	$2.25
☐	21699	**Rachel's Confession** #107	Fayrene Preston	$2.25
☐	21716	**A Tough Act to Follow** #108	Billie Green	$2.25
☐	21718	**Come As You Are** #109	Laurien Berenson	$2.25
☐	21719	**Sunlight's Promise** #110	Joan Elliott Pickart	$2.25
☐	21726	**Dear Mitt** #111	Sara Orwig	$2.25
☐	21729	**Birds Of A Feather** #112	Peggy Web	$2.25
☐	21727	**A Matter of Magic** #113	Linda Hampton	$2.25
☐	21728	**Rainbow's Angel** #114	Joan Elliott Pickart	$2.25

Prices and availability subject to change without notice.

Buy them at your local bookstore or use this handy coupon for ordering: